I0626476

The Oddfather

The Oddfather

Sol Weinstein & Howard Albrecht

Combustoica
a prose project of About Comics - Camarillo, California

IN MEMORIAM

ROBERT ALBRECHT
Who understood and should have seen it.

JOE E. LEWIS
King of the nightclubs, who, when he died, probably told God:
"I can hardly wait to hear what I'm gonna say next."

IRV WURZEL

YETTA CRAVITZ

JAMES GARRETT
Of the Cleveland *Press*.

MARSHALL MEHLWORM

THE CHARACTERS IN THIS BOOK ARE WHOLLY FICTIONAL. ANY
RESEMBLANCE, BY NAME OR OTHERWISE, TO PERSONS LIVING OR
DEAD IS PURELY COINCIDENTAL, ACCIDENTAL, OR TYPOGRAPHICAL.

Copyright 1973 by Sol Weinstein and Howard Albrecht. All
rights reserved.

Published by Combustoica, an imprint of About Comics.
www.Combustoica.com

2014 edition

DEDICATION

ELLEE, DAVID and JUDI WEINSTEIN; BERNICE, SHELLEE and RICHARD ALBRECHT.

SAM and CHAI SOORA WEINSTEIN, DR and MRS. HOWARD S. FRIEDMAN and BELKE, SETH and JOEL, ADA ALBRECHT, JANET, JERI and STEVEN ALBRECHT, TEDDY and EDDY ALBRECHT, STUART and PRISCILLA ALBRECHT, JOE and HANNA FREEDLAND, JOE and CYLVIA ALDERMAN, HARRY and BESS EISNER, MR and MRS. STAN EISNER, MRS. MARY GENTILE, H. J. SHERMAN, STEVE and JANET LEVINSON.

SHELDON KELLER
Our beloved mentor of mishigaas.

MARIO PUZO
Who knows that behind every great fortune is a crime... and behind every successful book two wild-eyed, slavering, rip-off parodists.

BILL (MR. L.A.) KENNEDY and his EVE
Of the Los Angeles *Herald-Examiner.*

RONN OWENS
Of WERE, Cleveland. Older, brasher, but so what?

SAUL ILSON and ERNEST CHAMBERS
Our beloved Bobby Darin Amusement Company producers.

JULIE ILSON and VERONICA DEE CHAMBERS
Their beloved producers.

GODFREY CAMBRIDGE

JACK McKINNEY
Of the Philadelphia *Daily News*, a man of many parts, all working... "The Sensuous Irishman."

CHARLES PETZOLD and TOM FOX
Of the Philadelphia *Daily News.*

ROSE (SAM) DeWOLF
Of the Philadelphia *Bulletin*, Vitamin E with legs. And her BERNIE INGSTER.

DORIS DAY, BUDDY HACKETT, MILTON BERLE, JOEY and SYLVIA BISHOP, TONY CURTIS, TIMMIE (OH YEAH!) ROGERS and BARBARA, LOUIE and ANITA NYE, ALLAN and WANDA DRAKE, SID and VANDA GOULD, CARL and ESTELLE REINER, PHIL FORD and MIMI HINES, BARRY SHEAR, TOMMY SANDS, MARTY and FRENCHY ALLEN, MEL FRANK, NORMAN PANAMA, TONY WEBSTER, BOB and EILEEN WEISKOFF, BOB and SABRINA SCHILLER, JERRY HELLER, BITSY, JAMIE and CASEY KELLER, MARTY SINGER.

LOU MARSH and TONY ADAMS
The Dons of the Comedy Box, Barcelona Hotel, Miami Beach.

JAN MURRAY, PAT HENRY, MORTY GUNTY, MARTY PASETTA, HAL and ELLIE ROSS, RICHARD ROTH, GEORGE DISKANT, MACK GRAY, MORT LACHMAN, HENRY (RED) MANDEL, ANNE MENNA, JOSH SHERMAN, CLARA SHERMAN, ART and SHULAMITH RUTKOFF, JAKE and DORIS SHERMAN, MOLLY LEVINE, DR. YEHUDA SHERMAN, JACK and MARY SHERMAN, MILLIE SCHOENBAUM, JOHNNY and HELEN BIENSTOCK, GLORIA WOLFORD, MICHAEL and CAROLINE ELIAS, GORDON and LYNN FARR, ARNOLD KANE, JERRY SCHOENBAUM, FRANK SHAW, DELLA WASSERMAN, BETH UFFNER, LYNN SHANKS, LOIS, CLAUDIA, AMY and SCOTT SLOAN, MORTY and BETTY WEST, BERNIE

WEINTRAUB, PAUL WAYNE, MARVIN and EVELYN WINKLER, ROMAIN, CAROLE AXE, BOBBY WEINER, and AGNES, BEA and MARGE at Schwab's, Beverly Hills, Calif.

LES and GAIL ROBERTS
Of Sherman Oaks, Calif.

LOU JACOBI

EARL WILSON
With thanks for his support of top-drawer comedy.

NORTON MOCKRIDGE
Ditto.

ART HOPPE
A funny cat

BOBBY and ELAINE VAN, JOHN DADES, VICKI CHRISTOPHER, KAYE DIAL, ELLEN GEER, MORRIS and ELENA DIAMOND, DR. ERNIE WHITE, DR. JEROME BRISKIN, EDIE GLADSTONE, WILLIE and BESS DIAMOND, THEBE and COOKIE DRAZIN, HY and KITTY BERKOWTTZ, ELLIOT ALEXANDER, SONNY and MYLES GOLDBERG, EILEEN and CHUCK OLSEN, JOE and BARBARA GARRAN, HALL and BETTY HANSEN, SUZANNE HILTON, TONY HANDLER, STANLEY HILTZIK, JUDY ACKERMAN, CLAUDIA ANDERSON.

(continued on page 116)

CHAPTER ONE

O n an August day so oppressive and steamy that on New York City's liquefied Mulberry Street some pedestrians were treading tar, the black sedan pulled over to the curb. "This is close enough," the driver said tersely. "Good luck, Tulio."

Tulio, a squat, swarthy individual in a waiter's uniform with the words "Chicken Cacciatore Delight" on the lapel, hoisted the huge paper bucket onto his shoulder, stepped out onto the sidewalk and wended his way past a group of wizened alta cockerias—old men—sitting in the street, exchanging gossip and sucking on old boccie balls.

His partner safely on his way, the driver, a tall, hawk-faced man in a wilting business suit, cut the ignition, went around to the trunk, and from it extricated two leather cases. He walked briskly into the hallway of an apartment building and despite the heat vaulted up the fetid stairs with agile bounds into an empty flat on the second floor, which he had rented a day before. There he stationed himself by a window, opened one leather case, set up a tripod, and removed from the other the components of a high-powered Japanese rifle, the famed and deadly Cocka-Pishi, which in addition to its undeniable killing power contained a small but powerful transistor radio built into its stock. As he waited, he switched it on. Out poured the dulcet voice of WNEW disc jockey William B. Williams. "That was Wayne Newton's new one, 'Your Kisses Give Me Liplash,' Number 32 on the chart..."

A fun gun, the man smiled, caressing the muzzle with a lover's tenderness. He'd used this radio-rifle on other contracts. Once, while listening to the throbbing beat of the Jackson Five, he had gunned down the Detroit Six. Accompanied by a Beatles' blockbuster, he'd busted down a whole block in Chicago, his main target, Bugsi Bunni, the founder of the Joyboy Clubs, whom he'd gotten right in his cottontail. An Elvis Presley rocker had furnished him the background for the killing of Sister George, the leader of a Brooklyn lesbian gang, the Amboy Dikes, and most recently Carole King's "Too Late, Baby" had been the all-too-true accompaniment to the slaying of San Francisco's Chinese-Italian mob kingpin, Ricearoni. Yes, a fun gun. While waiting to make a hit, you could hear a hit.

Through the telescopic sight, he could easily scan the bustling street activities. On a doorstep were the painted women brazenly shouting to male passersby to sample their charms at Anselmo's house of pleasure, the *hookeria*. Next door to Anselmo's, quite logically, was the clinic of Stephano Zarillo, M.D., the *veedee-eria*, and on the corner the restaurant of Pasquale Pascudnyaki, which, thanks to its highly seasoned bill of fare, was known as the *diarrhia*.

And across the narrow street, a scant thirty feet from his muzzle, was the mansion that dominated the neighborhood, the object of his patient vigil at the window. Soon he would get a fix on the leonine head that had been featured so often on the front page of the *Daily News,* usually ducking behind another front page of the *Daily News.* He would squeeze the trigger; that head would shatter into a mass of cranial splinters and gelatinous red matter, and in that instant, he would have fulfilled the contract of a lifetime, the murder of the Number One man of mobsterdom, the *baleboss foon alle di balebatim*, the boss of all bosses, the Godfather, Don Guido Provolone!

Tulio, the waiter, was nearing the tradesman's entrance to the mansion. Even as he had moved away from the sedan, he could see the hordes of young street toughs falling upon it like a school of piranhas; before he reached the comer of Mulberry and Hester, they'd already stripped it down to the chassis. An industrious bunch, he mused. Once he'd seen them at work at JFK Airport plundering a 747 jet just in from L.A., and in a twinkling they'd taken everything from the cockpit to twelve stewardesses. Good, he thought, let them have the car. The less evidence left the better.

Walking through the entrance, he found his arms pinioned by two muscular men in black suits and yellow ties, who gave him a fast, thorough frisking.

They were Nunzio Fresca and Renzo Uncola, the Don's oldest allies, whose stars had risen with Provolone's. Each commanded an army of *soldati* who at the drop of a gray fedora would swing into bloody action. Both had become fabulously wealthy in their own right under the Don's tutelage, Nunzio garnering his riches from a monopoly on soybean pancakes and Renzo from a monopoly on Monopoly sets, unbeknownst to the Parker Brothers.

"He's clean, Nunzio."

"Hold on, Renzo. Look in the bucket," Nunzio commanded and for a moment Tulio's heart thumped in *tarantella* time. Renzo lifted the lid, poked around, sniffed at the contents, and couldn't resist pilfering and nibbling a crisp wing. "Go ahead, buddy."

"Grazie," the waiter said humbly. A faint smile crinkled his lips as he walked into the huge garden, festooned with banners and flowers and thrumming with activity. The fools! They'd completely missed the .45 caliber famed and deadly Hunt & Wesson automatic in the bottom of hi bucket because it had been cleverly breaded to look and smell like a chicken leg, but Tulio knew how finger-lickin' lethal it would prove at the moment of truth, the moment when he emptied it into the heart of Fungi Provolone, the Don's eldest son.

On this joyous occasion, arranged to honor Fungi for achieving an exalted status in the Family, the Don was, according to ancient custom, disposed to grant favors to a stream of supplicants standing at the oaken doors to his den. One by one, they were led in by Lazar Pinsky, the elfin, mysterious Hebrew known as the *calculatori*, the calculator, who despite his alien heritage had become the Don's most trusted adviser, so often had he proved himself invaluable in matters of shrewdness and judgment.

Tramontana the tailor, an old friend whom the Don greeted with the pun, "You keep me in stitches," had been given a few hundred *lire* so that he could buy a new *Singeroni* sewing machine. Forza, the midtown pasta manufacturer, had entered with a tale of woe. The Board of Health, upon discovering ground-up rodentia in his macaroni, had threatened to close his establishment. A quick telephone call by the Don had closed the Board of Health.

"Bring in the next freeloader—uh—supplicant," Don Provolone said.

"He is here already," the *calculatori* stated. "Tino Shrimperini..."

"Ah, yes, my unhappy little friend, Tiny Tino. Where are you, Tino?"

"Here, great Don," squeaked a voice, "in your hand," and the Don quickly dropped what he had initially assumed was a Corona Corona cigar.

"Thank heaven, I did not light you," the Don told the twelve-inch-high little man who had once been the toast of three continents as a member of the famed but unfortunate circus family, the Falling Facendas. When the last of the Facendas had literally hit the bottom, Tiny Tino had found himself jobless and destitute.

There had been a little income here and there: male model for the Good Old Golden Rule Ruler Company, but another midget had unscrupulously inched him out of his job; then another temporary position as a bookmark for the collection of a wealthy bibliophile had ended in a near tragedy when Tino had been almost crushed to death in the middle of a Morocco-bound copy of "War and Peace"; and finally he answered a call from the Motion Picture Academy which, finding itself one Oscar short, had bronzed Tino and presented him to a fading movie queen, who had not kept him on her mantle but utilized him for lecherous purposes. During the course of this affair, he had been smitten by her, but had been advised by a friend to end the romance. "Tino, you're going in way over your head."

Before the pitiful midget could even begin his plea, the understanding Don pressed a crisp one thousand-dollar bill into his hand, and Tiny Tino immediately wrapped it around his lower body as though it were a bath towel.

"No, no," Don Provolone chided him gently. "It is for spending, not for wearing."

"Oh, my Don, a million thanks, not so much for me as for my baby brother, Little Lupo, whom I'm putting through theological college."

"Little Lupo, a priest?" the amazed Don said.

"No. Upon graduation, he will be a St. Christopher medal. And for your boundless generosity, some day, I, Tiny Tino, will return the favor."

The Don chuckled as he bade him farewell. Tiny Tino barely made it out of the den, almost falling prey to hungry Garibaldi, the Don's pet cat, but a quick kick by the Don in the feline's striped rump made him think better of it

Then Lazar Pinsky had whispered fiercely, pointing to the last name on the list of supplicants, a name circled in red ink. "He's in the garden. In disguise, of course. But first there is the matter of Lavagetto."

"Come in, old friend," boomed the Don's deep voice.

Trembling and terrified, Ignatio Lavagetto, the old cobbler, looked down upon his newly polished Keds, ill at ease in his frayed but well-laundered Robert Hall suit. His eyes seemed afraid to meet those of the man he called Godfather, the bulky man behind the mahogany desk. From the garden the musicians broke into a wild, unfettered, Sicilian groin-kicking dance whose strains could be heard all the way to 23rd Street, for the Don on this most festive of days had flown in the entire 250-piece Milano Symphony Orchestra, the Papal Tabernacle Choir, the Count Di Basi band and, as a gesture to the younger element among his followers, the prestigious rock group, the Rolling Minestrones.

Don Provolone, resplendent in a white Palm Beach suit and necktie which bore the Family crest, two crossed stilettos on a field of cheese, smiled. "Do not be timid in my presence, old compadre. You and I have shared many a glass of Geritoli together; we have labored side by side in my vineyards pressing the grapes; we have sat on stools swabbing each other's feet with Lysol to remove the purple stains. Yours, I perceive, are still purple, but that is the way of life, no? Now, tell me what brings a frown to your honest workman's face on this glad afternoon of my life and how can I, your Don, be of service to you?"

When Lavagetto neared the desk, the Don, as if in reassurance, patted his arm and somehow found his fingers closing around the old cobbler's wallet, which he hastily returned with an apologetic chuckle. "It is hard to break the habits of a lifetime."

Lavagetto began haltingly. 'I would hardly dare broach the matter except that it concerns someone exceedingly precious to me, my only daughter, Teresa..."

As he stammered out his words, there was a rapid flurry of iron pellets whizzing from his mouth. Don Provolone instinctively ducked behind his desk, shuddering, until the fusillade had ceased.

"A thousand pardons," Lavagetto said sheepishly. "I have been in the cobbler's trade so long, I frequently forget to remove the shoe tacks from my mouth. It is also hard for me to break the habits of a lifetime. I fear I have marred your priceless painting."

In a cold sweat, the August heat to the contrary, the Don rose and peered at the canvas of the Mona Lisa on the back wall of his den. Where formerly she had been smiling her enigmatic smile, there was now an expression of sheer horror and pain, for Lavagetto's volley of shoe tacks had riddled her chest.

"What is a two-million-dollar painting between friends? Go on, Lavagetto."

"Last night Teresa attended a dance at St. Agnes of the Rafflebook, where the dear, pious girl is the lead baritone in the choir. During the course of the evening, she met and was lured from the social hall by a young man... a *degenerati*." A look of animal fury was purpling the stoical old cobbler's face. "This man forced her into the back seat of his Jaguar and committed upon her sweet, virginal person indignities of the grossest sort." He clenched his fists; another volley of shoe tacks came jetting out of his mouth. The Don again ducked in time, but Garibaldi, his pet cat, did not escape the force of Lavagetto's mini-projectiles. The creature was neutered on the spot.

"Sweet Teresa violated so flagrantly? A terrible tragedy, indeed. Pray continue." The Don, touched as he was by the old cobbler's doleful narrative, nevertheless hoped he would get to the point before the den ended up looking like a certain garage in Chicago on that infamous St. Valentine's Day.

"Now, great Don, you and I are men of the world. We understand what may transpire when a hotblooded swain works his will upon a maid. But this... this *scumatori* went beyond the bounds of normality."

"Shocking."

"In his unbridled lust, not a single orifice on Teresa's body was left unsullied, not an aperture escaped the thrusting of his monstrous organ. This beast made penile penetrations in anatomical locations where none existed previously."

"I am appalled. How badly did the girl fare?"

"This morning when Teresa drank a cup of Folger's instant coffee, served to her, incidentally, by a strange Scandinavian woman named Mrs. Olson who has been appearing at our apartment for curious reasons known only to herself because neither of us knows her... this morning when Teresa drank the coffee, the total effect was like looking at liquid escaping through Swiss cheese. Teresa has become a living Fountain of Trevi... a human shower bath."

Now the Don got up to place a consoling arm upon his stricken friend's shoulder. And also to get out of range of his mouth. When the man across the street got his first glimpse of the magnificent head, he swung his Cocka-Pishi around a few degrees. There! Another movement would bring the Don exactly into the center of the gunsight.

"How," asked the Don, "may I assist you in wreaking vengeance upon this *rapatori*... this loathsome despoiler?"

Across the street the finger tightened on the trigger.

Lavagetto turned his head toward the window and lifted up his chin. "I would humbly request that you ask your son, Fungi, to *stop raping my daughter.*"

Blurting out his request ultimately proved too much. The shoe tacks he had been trying to hold in check flew out of his lips; there was the smashing of glass as they passed through the Don's window on a high, whining trajectory; then another sound of smashing glass as they bombarded the second story window across the street. Both men recoiled when they heard a horrible, trailing scream and witnessed a body plummeting from the tenement, striking the sidewalk with a crunching thump. The killer's prediction of cranial splinters and pulpy brain matter came true in a horrible instant, but they were his, not Don Provolone's. After him tumbled the tripod and the Cocka-Pishi, which bounced off a vendor's pushcart and sent lemon ices cascading into the faces of some FBI men in a parked Chevrolet nearby.

A great hubbub erupted outside. Old women in black shawls encircled the broken form now staining the cement. Seconds later, Nunzio and Renzo hauled the cadaver and his armaments into the Don's den through a secret side door and placed them on the carpet. The eyes had been skewered with ghastly accuracy by Lavagetto's last spray of flechettes.

"I know this man," Nunzio said. "He was Rocco the Rifle from Detroit, a hit man. He had you set up, Godfather, and if it were not for these shoe tacks..."

"Here's the rifle," Renzo broke in breathlessly.

The Don looked at the remnants of the weapon that had come so close to taking his life. From the stock a voice said, "That was Barbra Streisand singing her way from her nose into your heart." He snapped off the radio.

"Lavagetto, old *goombah*, your Don is greatly in your debt. I promise that my son will never again violate your darling Teresa. Here," and he shoved a stack of gold coins into the cobbler's hands, "buy enough Silly Putty to plug up any unsightly holes in her anatomy. And because you saved me from this *assassinatori*, I shall see to it that you have enough work to last you a lifetime. I shall draft a document granting you the concession to fix all the shoes of the entire New York City police department, until the day you die. In return, I would ask one small favor of you." As he spoke, he prudently crouched behind a large padded chair.

"A favor for a favor. That is the way of our clan, is it not?" the cobbler said, sending a squadron of tacks into the kneecaps of Nunzio and Renzo, who fled the den muttering dark curses.

"Promise me that starting now, you will never again utter a word in my presence."

The old cobbler began to swear his undying fealty, but the Don wisely pressed a copy of a best-selling novel against Lavagetto's mouth and felt the tacks slash through the cover, wounding Alexander Portnoy—right in his bathroom. Now Portnoy would really have something to complain about. The cobbler knelt and kissed the Don's great gleaming gold ring emblazoned with the letters Lucky Luciano High School of the Arts & Sciences and backed deferentially out of the room.

With a toe, the Don rolled over the body of the fallen foe. This creature had dared to end the existence of the great Don Provolone. Who had supplied the money for the contract? Who was challenging his majesty as the leader of the Families of the country? Certainly an immediate consultation with Lazar Pinsky, the *calculatori*, was in order.

On his way out of the den, he caught his reflection in the mirror and noticed with distaste that the harrowing events of the day had left his face thin and drawn. He could not present himself to his guests looking so haggard. To restore his visage to its fullness and authority, he reached into a drawer, took out several dozen sheets of Kleenex, and stuffed them into his shrunken cheeks. Excellento! The mirror now revealed a man with a full, imposing face, a man to be feared and respected —and that was good. True, the constant wedging of Kleenex into his cheeks sometimes hampered his speech, but had not the celebrated *actori* Marlon Brando built an entire and profitable career upon mumbling?

Confident once more, the Don walked into the sun and moved among the celebrants, pinching a black olive here, a piece of garlic bread there, a saucy female behind wherever one presented itself, drawing clucks of approval from his wife, the fullbreasted Contadina, a woman famed for her insuperable tomato paste, who sat fanning her face against the heat of the day with an old copy of the Kefauver Report on Crime.

He smiled to see his three fine sons enjoying themselves. There was Fungi, his thirty-year-old, soon to be accorded the signal honor of the day for his valorous conduct. He was a tall, broadshouldered lad whose black curly hair glinted in the rays of the sun, Fungi of the awesome *peckeroni*, the male sex organ, which reportedly started below his waist, dipped past his knees and invariably ended up in a cocktail waitress in Fort Lee, New Jersey. A good lad, but, alas, one who let his lechery and lust overrule his good judgment. Even as the Don gazed upon Fungi, he could perceive the lad was in a state of arousal while flirting with Angelina, the baker's daughter. Although Fungi's hands were at his side, the table at which he sat was already twelve inches off the floor and still rising as he whispered sweet obscenities into her ear. Watching the lad's obvious excitement, the Don recalled the day of Fungi's birth at Our Lady of the Overcharge Maternity Hospital. The nurses had come away from Contadina's bedside chuckling with disbelief at the display of manhood already apparent upon the ten-pound infant, seven pounds, six ounces of which constituted his *peckeroni*. Several of the nurses had already filed away Fungi's name for future reference, and by the age of eight the lad had been through more starched uniforms than LaFrance Blueing.

Ah, that organ of Fungi's! And what athletic prowess! During the lad's successful career in Little League ball, he had more than once driven towering home-runs over the centerfield fence— without taking a bat to the plate. Ah, that organ of Fungi's! Even now, while the lad whispered hot proposals into Angelina's ear, Rosetta-—two seats away —was receiving the fringe benefits. But could such a lad, however masculine, be entrusted to head the Family when, as all men must, the Don would go to the Last Hideout?

Perhaps the mantle of the Donship would fall upon the shoulders of his second son, Carmine, now twenty-eight. True, the lad was a good son, loyal and loving, but would the Don's far-flung organization respect a leader whose favorite TV program was "Ding Dong School" and who, when all the others at Family business meetings were garbed in camel's-hair coats and gray fedoras, came in wearing Dr. Denton pajamas, bouncing a pink Spaulding rubber ball and repeating in cadence, "My name is Carmine... and my wife's name is Cathy... we come from California... and we sell coconuts..."

No, it would not be Carmine, the Don decided.

Which left only Nicholas, twenty-five, whose face, although dark and vivid in coloration like his older brothers', did not possess their sensual brutality but rather a refinement and softness which set him apart. While Fungi and Carmine were playing their rough street games... mugging buses, playing hopscotch (which involved smoking hop and drinking scotch), hide-and-seek (in their version they hid in local shops after hours so they would have ample time to seek the cash register), Nicholas had displayed an artistic bent. He had gone to Young People's Concerts conducted by Leonard Bernstein, who had explained Beethoven to the children, and then after the concerts Nicholas had stood in the lobby explaining Leonard Bernstein to the children, sometimes to Leonard Bernstein. He had majored in music at Juilliard and one night had brought joy to the Don's heart when he walked into the mansion carrying his violin case—evoking great memories of the Don's apprenticeship during Prohibition. But, alas, he'd shattered the old man's fantasy when he opened the case to display nothing more than a real violin.

But still the blood of the Provolones coursed through his veins and on the day when Nicholas had returned from a local movie house featuring a sadistic Richard Widmark picture and had emulated the star by pushing an old woman in a wheelchair down six flights of stairs, the Don had rejoiced: "There's good stuff in the boy, after all."

Suddenly there was a chorus of screaming throughout the garden. For an instant the Don thought Lavagetto had broken his vow of silence and had opened his mouth, but then he saw the women, young and old, their hands clasped to their breasts, sighing and swooning. Into the throng, his gold lamé tuxedo flashing in the sun, strode the famed singing idol, a boy from the old neighborhood who had won his initial fame under his own name of Vic Di-Romanci.

Ah, the Don thought, he has not forgotten his roots; he is a true Godson. Happily he watched his protege moving through the adoring females, stealing a kiss here, an apartment key there, and his mind journeyed back to the curlyheaded choirboy whose voice had sweetly pierced the Sunday morning masses at Our Madonna of the Bingo Card on Sullivan Street. How far Vic had progressed from his humble beginnings as a member of the local folksinging combo, Peter, Paul and Mario, (for a year Vic had been Mario, after Mario somehow had convinced Motown to make him a Supreme). In those days Vic had been lucky to earn five dollars a night singing at Bar Mitzvahs, which in this neighborhood were understandably infrequent, but made up for it by singing at gangland funerals, which happily were not.

His first big break had come by winning the Mick Mack Amateur TV Hour with a sensitive rendition of "Alley Oop," which had convinced the Don to give him his first recording session on Knuckle Records, one of the Provolone enterprises. He had set a million teen hearts aflutter with his first disc smash:

Sophomore Prom,
Wabba-da-babba-da-babba-da-babba-da

Sophomore Prom,
Wabba-da-babba-da-babba-da-babba-da...

Then followed it up quickly with another million-seller:

Junior Prom,

Wabba-da-babba-da-babba-da-babba-da...

And when the cynical musical pundits had kissed him off as a two-hit flash-in-the-pan, he'd reached into the core of his creative genius and plucked out his third consecutive gold record:

Senior Prom,
Wabba-da-babba-da-babba-da-babba-da...

But then the day of the Italian crooner began to wane. "That old swoon stuff is out," Vic had told his benefactor. "There's a new music coming out of the British Isles, and I've got to change with the times." The Don had agreed and invested a fortune in reshaping Vic Di-Romanci's image. He had been sent to Wales to saturate himself in this profitable new musical culture. There he not only learned the difficult, jaw-breaking language and their sound and rhythm but so assiduously did he apply himself to the Welsh folkways that he returned with a severe case of black lung and a fear of caverns. And so he burst anew on the American scene with his Carnaby Street Mod apparel, his altered singing style, and his catchy new name—Engelbrute Pumpernickel!

Now there were cries of "Sing, Engelbrute, sing!" and the young man motioned to the 340 musicians and they adlibbed background music as he swung into one of his immortal hits, sending flashes of desire through previously blocked varicose veins and melting support hose as he crooned:

Ifs fairly usual to have fun with anyone,
Dee, dee, dee, dee, dee, dee,
But when her husband pulls out a gun, it's time
   to run,
Dee, dee, dee, dee...

A sock hit, indeed, the Don knew, but the last one Engelbrute had enjoyed for two years. Because of his liaisons with wanton women, his carousing, his tippling, his incessant smoking of cigarettes (alas, his voice had found no happiness in Marlboro Country), the old Engelbrute pipes had gone bad and now he was a shell of his former self. In order to restore his fading name, he had accepted the starring roles in a series of cheaply made movies: the disastrous motorbike film, "Hernia on a Honda"; the equally disastrous Italian Western, "A Fistful of Fettuccini"; and his latest cinematic catastrophes, the horror movie science-fiction series: "The Planet of the Chickens," "Behind the Planet of the Chickens," "Scooping Up The Droppings from the Planet of the Chickens," all box office flops which *Variety*, the show business journal, had referred to in a typical headline: CHIX PIX UP CRIX!

Despite his personal misfortunes he had taken the time to leave the heartbreak of Hollywood (where he had also picked up the heartbreak of psoriasis from a maiden of dubious personal hygiene) to return to his Godfather's mansion and pay homage to his old street buddy, Fungi, on the latter's big day. This had pleased the Don—the lad had not forgotten the Family or the obligation to show respect. He would do something for Engelbrute if he could.

In the midst of Engelbrute's next song, "Oh, Release Me"—

> *Oh, Release Me, darling do,*
> *I'm half dead from loving you,*
> *You're a tiger in the sack,*
> *Oh, Release Me, before you break my back!*

the Don motioned to the tiring balladeer who happily cut the song short before he was forced to hit the high-C his ailing voice could no longer tackle. Indeed, in these dark days of the Engelbrute Pumpernickel saga, the only Hi-C he had been in contact with was a fruit drink, which he laced with gin.

Now they were in the Don's den, stepping over the body of Rocco the Rifle, which the Don's hirelings had neglected to take away. Perhaps I shall leave it there for a while, the Don thought. It gives the room a certain stylistic flair.

They embraced and he poured his erring Godson a tall glass of Kool-Aidanti, a domestic but tasteful vintage from his own cellar.

"My son, you look tired. Things have not been going well in the great Land of Fantasy in the West?"

"To the outward world, yes, my great Don. No doubt you have seen mentions of my name in the columns of such Hollywood reporters as Rona Borax, Sidney Schlocksy and Joyce Jabber, always in connection with some great project, some great movie, some TV series, but these are just items put in by my press agent whom I cannot even afford to pay twenty dollars a week anymore. But in reality, since wine, women and bad songs have taken their toll of my voice, I can't get a decent nitery engagement; film producers shun me; TV executives do not answer my pleas. I called my agent for work... any work... but he put me on hold in July of 1970 and I've been waiting by the phone ever since. Things are so bad that even callgirls don't call back."

"I know all this, my foolish Vic, or Engelbrute, if you prefer. And I am once again prepared to help the angelic choirboy I knew so long ago."

Engelbrute took a stubbed-out Old Gold cigarette from his pocket, flattened it out, lit up its burnt end, and let its acrid smoke further irritate the worn and frayed throat lining that should have been replaced at his forty-thousand-song checkup. "Oh, Godfather, how can I again ask for your help after all you have done for me?"

"Ask, my Godson, and if it is within my power, I shall grant it." The Don noticed that without the sun's rays even the gold lamé tuxedo was tarnishing.

"Have you ever heard of Wally Dizzy?"

"Ah, yes." The Don smiled. "Who has not heard of Wally Dizzy, whose cartoon characters have delighted millions of children throughout the world to the point where he has constructed an empire of happiness... a multi-million-dollar Dizzyland in Hollywood, another in Chicago, another in Miami.

"How I, like so many others, have laughed at the rollicking antics of Dizzy Duck, the cartoon clown who launched him on his way to becoming a legend in his own time. And after Dizzy Duck came Happy Hippo, Wacky Wombat, Zippy Zebra, Poopy Porcupine. Then Contadina and I, during the terrible days of the Brooklyn bloodbath during which we wiped out the Cannolli gang, often relaxed from a day of massacre by enjoying Wally Dizzy's full-length feature cartoons, "Gumbo, the Flying Shrimp," "Finocchio, the Little Blue Fairy," and "Cavity, the Tooth Fairy."

Engelbrute inhaled again, a mite too deeply, for now he had used up the last shred of tobacco and was smoking the filter. Six more polyps popped out of his aching throat. "But now Mr. Dizzy has begun to make films using live actors, and they, too, have been box office smashes. I need not remind you of such high-grossing flicks as 'The Gorilla That Wore Wedgies,' 'The Whale That Was Elected to Congress,' 'The Armadillo Who Became an Astronaut,' and so many more. I have learned from a secretary in his office who enjoys my short hand as much as I enjoy hers that he is about to embark upon his most riotous comedy, 'The Nun That Kicked a Computer.' Oh, Godfather, there's a marvelous part in that film that could bring me back to the top, the role of Hermes the shepherd boy... and it's so perfect for me. I wouldn't even have to act. I could just play myself. After all, who knows more about sheep than a Sicilian?"

Who else indeed? the Don thought, remembering his own boyhood in the old country where sheep were for more than just herding. To this day he felt a pang whenever Contadina served him a lambchop. (A lost love in his own Summer of '42?) "The part most certainly would be a natural for you... or unnatural, as the case may be. Have you approached Mr. Dizzy concerning its availability?"

"Dammit, I can't even get through the Dizzy Studio gate. I know what they think in there. I'm too old, too hard-looking, a rotten actor. All of which is true, but what has that got to do with success in Hollywood?"

The Don pondered the problem for a moment. He walked over to his liquor cabinet and took out a bottle. "Here," and he poured Engelbrute a large glass. "It's the new sensation of New York— 'Crazy Gallo Wine.' You take a shot of it and it takes a shot at you. Let us toast to your success in this new movie."

"But," and Engelbrute looked hard at the Don, "Wally Dizzy is the most powerful mogul on the coast, even as you are on your turf. What if he refuses to give me the role?"

"I shall dispatch the *calculatori* to Los Angeles to talk to Mr. Dizzy... and if words fail, I shall send him a sign he can't decline."

"Oh, Don Provolone." The red-veined, sinbesotted eyes of Engelbrute flooded with tears. Ricking the body of Rocco the Rifle to one side, he fell to his knees and pressed his full, sensual mouth against the Don's ring. When a little tongue slipped out, the Don realized that Engelbrute, too, could not break the habits of a lifetime. Whistling happily—and of course, off-key—the singer left to rejoin the festivities. The Don shoved another hundred sheets of Kleenex into his mouth and followed him out.

The party was in full sway and Engelbrute again was swarmed by his shrieking claque and forced to croak his way past two choruses of another of his golden hits, "I Lost My Heart in San Francisco and My Stugazza in Pauline Piazza." Little men from the Chicken Cacciatore Delight catering service moved about with their heaping buckets, among them Tulio, who congratulated himself on blending in so well. Truly, this deception was proving profitable for not only would he receive 25 G's for the contract on Fungi, but he'd already made $10.60 in tips.

At a signal from the Don the symphony struck a fanfare and the crowd ceased its chattering. The moment had arrived. Responding to a clap of the Don's hands, Nunzio and Renzo wheeled out a gigantic, triple-tiered cheesecake made especially for the occasion by the world-renowned Kitchens of Sara Leoni, another of the Don's aboveboard enterprises.

"Fungi, where is Fungi?" the Don whispered to the *calculatori*. "The boy should be here to receive his reward."

Pinsky smiled. "If I know the lad's predilections, he is getting his reward at this very moment. Follow the sighs and you will find Fungi."

Angry at his son's childish dalliance at such a significant moment, the Don flashed a glowering glance at Nunzio, who immediately went back into the mansion, cocked an ear, picked up an all too familiar sound from an upstairs bedroom and followed his instincts.

"Oh, Fungi, Fungi!" Great wracking sobs of ecstasy tore from the throats of both Angelina and Rosetta, who were learning the meaning of the ancient proverb, "Share the rod... and spoil the child."

There was a sharp rap on the door. "It's me, Nunzio. The Godfather wants you downstairs on the double."

"I'm on the double upstairs," Fungi panted, and with a fantastic maneuver that would have caused envy in a Roto-Rooter repairman, brought the two girls to their simultaneous climax. Giving each a final kiss, he bounded downstairs after the sweating Nunzio.

At his reappearance he was greeted with thunderous applause and the ceremony began with the Don's opening remarks.

"Fungi, my son..." The Don coughed. A wad of Kleenex had lodged in his larynx. Swallowing it, he went on. "Fungi, this is a proud day for the Provolone clan. Last week in Philadelphia in Santoro's Steakhouse you, by eliminating Musso the Muscle, Luigi the Lip, and Carlo the Claw, reached a shining plateau, your one hundredth killing."

Great cheers cascaded throughout the garden. Tulio, virtually unnoticed, moved closer to the giant cake, his hand slowly closing over the fake chicken leg.

"To mark this shining moment the *soldati* of the Family have all chipped in to buy you a little token of their esteem. Come forward, my son."

Fungi, his eyes ashine with excitement, did his father's bidding. Tulio, his Hunt & Wesson now fully out of the bucket, took another step toward Fungi. He nibbled off some of the breading from the gun barrel.

"Here, my son, to celebrate your prowess... a present we hope you will find worthy of your achievements..." From a velvet box in Renzo's hand the Don took out the gift and placed it tenderly in his son's strong, firm fingers.

Fungi's eyes welled. What sentimentality, what thoughtfulness! This Family, which society had deemed cruel and heartless, had the good taste to present him with a golden icepick.

Immediately the crowd was on its feet, shouting "Viva! Viva!" and upon hearing this, Fungi's brother Carmine, his mind ever working in quirky ways, rushed over with a twenty-nine-cent roll of paper towels.

Now as Fungi stood near the cake, the tears raining down his brutally handsome face, Tulio moved within one foot of his quarry and raised his chicken leg.

"Oh, my father, I swear that I shall not be unworthy of this magnificent gift," Fungi said with true conviction. "I swear that." As he flung his arms out dramatically to emphasize his vow, there was a gasp from the throng, for Fungi had accidentally rammed the golden icepick deep into the heart of the little waiter on his right.

In his death throes Tulio squeezed the trigger, but the shot went awry and flew harmlessly into the rosebushes, wounding old Gregorio the gardener, who was pruning the Don's prize flower, "The Mrs. Miniveri Rose." Old warhorse that he was, Gregorio shrugged off the pellet in his shoulder, put the clippers in his other hand, and continued snipping away.

"*Momma Mia!*" the Don whispered to Pinsky. "This neighborhood is crawling with *assassinatoris!* Well, Fungi, my son, by your fortuitous thrust you have started on your way to the next plateau, a platinum icepick." Then he shouted. "Let us have mass merriment!"

The musicians took their cue and launched into a spirited folk dance. The guests followed suit, and after the removal of Tulio's body, gyrated wildly throughout the balance of the afternoon.

Though laughter reigned outside, the Don back in his den with his sons was tight-lipped and furious. "My sons, I am inured to the prospect of attempts on my life, but that someone should have tried to take yours, Fungi, as well makes the wine boil in these old veins. Do you have any thoughts on the matter?"

"I say we get plenty of ammo and start rubbing out anybody who gets in our way," was Fungi's immediate response.

The Don sighed. He had heard from Fungi exactly what he had not wanted to hear, an unthinking outburst of hotblooded temper, but no rational thought. Again he felt qualms about someday yielding his Donship to this foolhardy eldest son. "And you, Carmine... ?"

Carmine knitted his brows, thought a second, bounced his pink Spaulding, and said, "My name is Carmine... and my wife's name is Carole... we come from Chicago... and we sell corsets."

"I'm sorry I asked," the Don cut in. "And you, Nicholas?" His eyes raked the brooding countenance of his youngest son for some sign of leadership.

Nicholas went to the piano, played Tchaikovsky's Concerto in B-Minor, tugged at his earlobe, scratched his chin, pinched the bridge of his nose, furrowed his brows, and stroked his hair.

Viewing these actions, the Don had mixed emotions. Without question the lad had a cool, analytical mind with the patience to think out a problem, but he also had the worst spastic condition this side of the Mayo Clinic.

"I think there is a *conspiradetta* against us, Dad," Nicholas said quietly. He then fell silent and played the Peer Gynt Suite.

So, a conspiracy, the Don thought. But again, who?

Who had paid off Rocco the Rifle, Tulio the Trigger? It was unthinkable that the other Dons of the country would be involved in this heinous matter. He knew he enjoyed their esteem and respect. And yet, within his own New York empire, there had been a series of unexplained events, principally emanating from uptown: a bookie parlor dynamited on 117th at Seventh Avenue; a floating crap game sunk at 157th and Riverside Drive; and the still unsolved murder of his top Harlem moneylender, Mack the Shark. Were these all random and unrelated occurrences or the beginnings of a pattern that threatened his domain? He scowled, probing his mind for a possible clue, when the *calculatori* entered with his soft tread.

"Don Provolone. Let me remind you of the last supplicant on the list, the man who awaits you in the secret nook in the garden."

"I have no time for..."

The *calculatori* said, "For this man you must make time." He scribbled something on a notepad and held it under the Don's nose. The Don nodded and followed Pinsky to the quiet place under the vines.

The sun was going down now, a feeble attempt to match what Fungi was doing in a third-floor bedroom. The musicians were packing their instruments, the guests were saying their *buone seres*, the lights of Mulberry Street were beginning to twinkle.

The man hidden by the vines was dressed in the garb of a rough-hewn stone mason, his fingernails caked with red brick dust, a trowel sticking ostentatiously from the back pocket of his overalls. But as the Don approached him he knew that this individual was no member of his ethnic group, no matter how cleverly he had been outfitted. Instead of the earthy smells of pepper, zucchini and garlic customarily wafting from the body of an ordinary artisan, this man exuded the ungodly, distasteful (to the Don) essences of Velveeta Cheese, Miracle Whip mayonnaise, Wonder Bread and Skippy Peanut Butter.

And unlike the other supplicants who had sought his favor on this unusual day, this man would not bend to kiss the Don's ring. And the Don did not realistically expect this kind of obeisance from a man who wielded a power even mightier than his own, a man who commanded legions and armadas... a man who was the President of the United States.

CHAPTER TWO

"I am honored beyond words that you should be here today, sir," the Don said solemnly. "But if I may be so bold, what does the world's leading citizen... with the possible exception of Pat Cooper... wish with a humble Mulberry Street businessman?"

"You demean yourself, Don Prophylactic."

"Provo*lone*, gracious sir, if you please. May I offer you a cool drink on this sweltering evening?"

"Thank you, no," the President replied. "I already had a refreshing glass of Tang, the beverage favored by our brave astronauts, while I helicoptered to New York. I have always thought that since this is the only commercial drink ever served on the lunar surface, its makers should now call it Moon Tang. That's a little Presidential humor there, Don Provo... uh... Utah."

"Provo*lone*, sir. I am surprised you have such difficulty with my name. It surely should be well known to you for it occupies three floors worth of files at the FBI."

The President let that comment go by. He reached into his overalls and pulled out a fat link of pungent *sausigi*. The Don was pleased that the President had made an obvious effort to assimilate into what must have been, for him, strange surroundings.

"Would you care to join me?" the President asked, pulling another link of *sausigi* from his pocket and handing it to his host. But the latter dropped his to the ground when he saw his distinguished visitor place a gold Ronson to the tip of his and drag deeply on it in an effort to light it.

This man is merely trying to impress me with his knowledge of my heritage, but he has bungled it miserably, the Don thought bitterly. He wants something.

"Hah, hah," the President chuckled with bogus joviality, puffing away on the link. "You folks certainly know how to live."

"What can I do for you?" Don Provolone said, a sudden testiness in his voice.

"It is... uh... very difficult to know where to begin, Don Propensity."

The Don this time ignored the insulting mispronunciation of his noble surname. "May I suggest you begin at the beginning?"

"This great land, yours and mine, a land of mighty urban centers, purple-mountained majesties, great ranges where the deer and the antelope play "

"Cut the shit," the Don snapped, and the smoking sausigi fell out of the startled President's mouth.

"Very well, let me make this problem perfectly clear, and we do, indeed, have a problem, make no mistake about that. This country through a secret treaty is committed to the defense of a sundered Indochinese nation, the tiny subversion-racked land of Cheong-Sam. Our sympathies lie with General Phieu, the leader of the southern half of this nation, hereafter to be referred to as South Cheong-Sam."

"A brilliant choice of name for the southern half of the country," the Don interjected, "leaving the northern half, I suppose, to be entitled North Cheong-Sam."

A surprised look stole across the President's face. This allegedly humble businessman was no fool. "North Cheong-Sam is headed by a dedicated revolutionary known as Ho Ho Ho."

"These Orientals have quaint names," the Don commented.

"Actually, Ho Ho Ho is not his real name. Many years ago while studying in our Yale University, in order to pick up extra money he worked as a Santa Claus for a midtown department store. He became so enamored of Santa's jolly laugh that he dropped his given name and adopted Ho Ho Ho as his own. Now, in order to maintain our world prestige we must back the forces of General Phieu, an admitted ultra-right-wing fascist dictator who is moving opportunistically toward the political center as opposed to Ho Ho Ho, a diehard Communist despot who is gradually moving to the extreme right, albeit in a left-wing manner."

"You have, indeed, made it perfectly clear, Mr. President. Now, how may I assist you?"

"Though General Phieu cables our State Department daily for aid against the ever encroaching guerrilla movement of Ho Ho Ho, I dare not commit hundreds of thousands of men, planes, ships and materiel of all kinds. The American public, both hawk and dove, have been badly stung by our Vietnam misadventure and it would cost me my political life to immerse this nation again in an Asian land war. Even if I did reject the counsel of my closest advisers at State, there is the staggering financial problem, which our nation cannot afford at this time. My experts estimate that the defense of South Cheong-Sam would cost me no less than forty billion dollars a year."

"I can appreciate your problem, Mr. President, but how does it concern a man who wishes merely to grow a few roses, collect a few rents, run a few unions, dominate a few Congressmen, control the Eastern seaboard, buy a few million acres of land in California, Nevada, and New Mexico..."

"Wait!" The President halted the Don's statement of his humble aims in life. "You are exactly the man who can solve my enigma. From all I have heard of you and your methods, I want you and your organization to take on the defense of South Cheong-Sam. Naturally I do not expect you to do this without some sort of aid from me. I am fully prepared to lend you a few thousand men who have been training clandestinely for this project... Green Berets, Blue Berets, even Lavender Berets, should you meet resistance from Communist deviants. I can give you some PT boats, 'copters, artillery pieces... and the not inconsiderable sum of one billion dollars, which has been hidden from the Congress in a secret CIA conduit with the code name *Foundation for the Psychological Investigation of the Problems of the Emotionally Stable.*"

"I will accept the task. But I do not require the men, the money or the equipment."

"Then how can I repay you for such monumental patriotism? I know you have grave problems with the Internal Revenue Service. Can I intercede on your behalf?"

'It has been taken care of."

"Perhaps I can delay indefinitely the reconvening of the Congressional Committee on Organized Crime."

"It has been taken care of. Their next meeting is not scheduled until 1993."

"Can I stop the deportation of some of your close associates?"

"It has been taken care of. The ship turned around this morning and will dock in New York tomorrow."

"But there must be something I can do for you."

"There will come a day when I in turn will need a great boon and you must grant it without question for this is the way of our life—quid pro quo. But I do not expect a man who screws up a simple name like Provolone to understand what that means."

The President, knowing what the awful alternatives would be in this delicate matter of South Cheong-Sam, spoke quickly. "I accept. The favor will be yours."

As the two men shook hands to seal the compact, the Don saw a hollowness on the President's face, doubtlessly caused by his having to deal with a man whose world of lying, cheating and double-dealing differed so markedly from his own world of lying, cheating and double-dealing. "You look tired, Mr. President. If I may offer a suggestion, here"—he placed a bundle of Kleenex in the visitor's palm—"put these in your mouth and your face will again appear formidable."

The President grinned. "You do that shtick, too? My television makeup man does that to me every time I go on the tube. Farewell, Don Pro... hmm... hmmm... hmm." And he deliberately slurred the last syllables, an old trick often employed by politicians who could not remember their constituents' names.

He tiptoed out of the garden, climbed into a rickety truck and drove off down the twisting street. An excellent charade, the Don thought, probably arranged by a top-secret security organization. Soon the man would be met by a limousine, then helicoptered to the airport to the Presidential jet, flown to Washington, where he would be taken in another rickety truck to the White House.

Lazar Pinsky came out of the shadows. "It is a remarkable thing to have such a personnage in your debt, oh great Don, but have we not bitten off more than we can chew? How can we execute this contract without his men, his ships, his weaponry?"

"I have thought it out. Send for Bonfiglio Bucceroni."

The *calculatori* shrank in horror. "Of course. It is the only way. I shall call in 'The Butcher.' "

CHAPTER THREE

S alvatore Bucceroni stood in the corridor of Boss Tweed Memorial Hospital, his heart leaping with expectation, for Maria's time was nigh. Minutes ago his friend Alfredo had tugged him away from his pushcart where he had been crying out, "Tutsi-frutsi ice cream... getta you tutsi-frutsi ice cream!" and had led him into this fine American institution where soon he, a humble immigrant from Palermo, would be the father of a fine American child.

"This way, quickly!" said an orderly, leading him into a waiting room filled with other anxious fathers smoking cigarettes, pacing nervously, and goosing passing nurses—for they had long been deprived of the pleasures of womanhood.

There was a shriek from the labor room and he knew that Maria was about to disgorge her bundle. Subsequently, Maria gave another plaintive cry and into the world on July 12, 1926, surrounded by kindly Dr. Waldman, two nurses, and the orderly, plunged Bonfiglio Bucceroni. "He appears to be a magnificent specimen," Dr. Waldman told the ashen-faced Maria, giving the doughty buttocks a slap. A red fire of anger blazed in the infant's eyes and he kicked out savagely at his tormentor, landing a crashing blow to the physician's midsection, driving him back into a rack of scalpels, three of which pierced kindly Dr. Waldman's back.

Lashing out again and again, the irate infant's pistonlike legs connected against vital organs, and soon the doctor was joined in death by the two nurses and the orderly. And so on that day in July the fate of Bonfiglio Bucceroni was sealed, his destiny in life assured. He would be a superb instrument of murder.

The passing years proved this prophecy. In the streets of downtown Manhattan there were to be three infamous street gangs terrorizing the inhabitants... the fifteen-member aggregation known as the Muldoon gang, forty-

five toughs who called themselves the Melnick gang, and
the most fearsome, dangerous and murderous of all, the
Bucceroni gang, of which Bonfiglio was the sole member.
And by the time he was ten, he was the sole gang.

In an effort to assuage the young man's hostile,
antisocial attitudes, the Herald Tribune Fresh Air Fund
collected $5,000 in door-to-door solicitations from a more
than willing neighborhood, which was disappointed to
learn that "The Butcher," as he now was known, was only
to be sent to a summer camp in the nearby Adirondacks,
and not the Belgian Congo as they had hoped. Two days
later an upstate New York newspaper carried a frightening
story of a camp decimated by some strange force: six
counselors garrotted with volleyball nets, four former
Olympic swimming champions found drowned in a foot of
water, the iron cots bent into pretzels, and twelve acres of
rich timber burned to stumps.

His teen years witnessed a similar slew of carnage, but
by this time the young man had become more refined in
his techniques, familiarizing himself with Karate, kung fu,
savate, the use of the Polynesian war club, the Australian
boomerang (once using it so proficiently that it feared
to return to the hands of its owner), the machete, the
pitchfork, the gaucho bolas, the Thuggee strangling cord,
various types of explosives, and even the difficult-to-master
Scottish Highland telephone-pole throw, the latter earning
him his first citation on the 19th Precinct Police blotter
because at the time he hurled it there was a repairman on
the top and also because he disconnected the entire service
of three of New York's five boroughs.

All of life's other vices—gluttony, women, drugs,
liquor—somehow had no place in "The Butcher's" life.
There was only the lust for blood. Hired by Tough Tommy
Placenta, a notorious waterfront boss, to keep order on
the violence-ridden docks, Bonfigjio, after singlehandedly
attacking and destroying a Liberty Ship on Pier 59, was
finally overwhelmed by 400 longshoremen, a cordon of
special riot police, and generous quantities of mustard
gas. Sent to Dannemora Prison, where he was given a term

of not less than three-and-a-half and not more than 150 years and shackled in a solitary confinement cell to a forty-ton block of cement with an anchor once used to hold the *Normandie,* Bucceroni's plight came to the attention of Don Provolone through the heartrending pleas of his parents. "He is a good boy," Salvatore said beseechingly. And the Don, with the machinations of Lazar Pinsky, a battery of legal eagles, and a promise to get the governor's son off heroin and back onto speed where he belonged, was not only able to free Bonfiglio but find a place for him in his organization.

Eternally grateful for his freedom, "The Butcher" realized that brute strength alone was not the end-all, that the power of a man like the Godfather was to be acknowledged and respected. For the first time in his violent life he genuflected before another human being, kissed the Don's ring, and vowed his everlasting loyalty.

Now the Don waited in his den for his one-man destruction team, glancing at his watch. The appointment was for midnight, and sure as the clock chimed twelve in the steeple of the Metropolitan Life Insurance Building, there was a thunder that shook the mansion.

With a strident crash "The Butcher" made his usual entrance into the den—through the wall. Thank heaven, I am also in the construction business, the Don thought.

He wasted no time. Pulling out a map of Indochina, he spoke rapidly to "The Butcher," who nodded at various intervals. "It is understood?" the Don asked. "It is done," The Butcher answered and left by way of another wall.

CHAPTER FOUR

It was 11 P.M. on September 15th and the usual clamor on heavily traveled Route 4 in Paramus, New Jersey, had begun to diminish drastically. The Garden State residents who had crossed the George Washington Bridge into New York to catch the doubleheader at Yankee Stadium had recrossed the span on their way back to their nests in surburbia, their cars loaded with souvenirs of the twin bill, which the once glorious Yankees had dropped to the Milwaukee Brewers, 19-1 and 23-2. Because the Bronx Bombers' fates had fallen so low since the golden days of Ruth, DiMaggio and Mantle, the management had sought to fight the declining attendance by offering "Ball Night," "Bat Night," and "Hat Night." This evening, in a strenuous bid for a sellout, they had instituted "Player Night," during which nine lucky scorecard holders were given the Yankees' starting team. The event had drawn 2,410, of whom 1,965 were nonpaying servicemen and members of Knothole Gangs.

With the closing of the great shopping centers, Route 4's only late-night attractions were the hum of the neon signs flashing "Vacancy" on its hundreds of roadside motels, in whose cubicles cavorted all the "John Smiths" between Teaneck, New Jersey, and Spring Valley, New York, none of whom spent more than ninety minutes in a room. Because of this nocturnal activity, the motels nightly used up more sheets (and, in the eyes of many, for a better purpose) than the Ku Klux Klan had worn in its entire history.

One nonsexual establishment was still open, with an hour of business left to transact. It was a MacDonaldi's, one of several hundred hamburger stands dotting the nation, still attracting patrons with its national symbol, the two fallen arches.

At 11:01 P.M. a block-long Cadillac El Dorado swerved off the superhighway into the parking lot and dimmed its lights. From the back seat stepped a portly, gray-haired man in a camel's-hair coat, a fedora pulled over his suntanned brow. On either side of him stalked his aides, one a man with a cheery childish expression associated generally with innocence, but those who had made the acquaintance of "Babyface" Gerber knew better. The other man, a lupine individual known as "Wolfman Jack," a definite top-forty killer, motioned. "It's all clear."

The chieftain slipped out of his camel coat, tossing it and the fedora into the limousine's back seat. Now he stood revealed in a typical MacDonaldi service uniform— white cutaway jacket, red slacks, and stiff, white, circular cardboard cap.

Walking across the spotless asphalt lot, he could not be distinguished from any other MacDonaldi employee, except perhaps for his age, the Luger bulging out of his jacket, and his $150 Gucci loafers.

He entered and was greeted immediately by the lone late-night counterman, the typically cheerful, polite and pimply sort hired for this kind of work. The youth looked at him for a moment, then glanced suspiciously at a portrait on the wall and cried, "Oh, my God... you're Mr. MacDonaldi! Oh, sir, what an honor to have you here in Paramus, but what have I done wrong? I swear I've been trying to push 'em so gosh dam hard, but nobody wants the new squidburgers."

"That's okay, son." Machiavelli (Mac) Donaldi, the founder of this nineteen-cent gold-mine chain, gave the lad a friendly wink. "It so happens that once a year I tour each one of my 365 joints and tonight it's Paramus's turn. I like to keep in touch with the customers, know what I mean? Now, you go home, Chester, and me and my... uh... account executives will finish up the night. Here, take a couple bucks, buy some Clearasil and work on the pimples, right, kid?"

The young man's 1959 Volkswagen burped out of the lot, but as he swung onto the road he blinked in disbelief to see a line of El Dorados, each as imposing as Mr. MacDonaldi's, entering the parking lot. "Gosh dam, Mr. MacDonaldi sure has a big bunch of account execs," he enthused.

The lot by now was jammed with other portly, gray-haired men, each flanked by his sinister looking advisers, each shedding his camel coat and fedora to expose the MacDonaldi uniform.

In three minutes the back counter was occupied by all the leading Dons in the United States.

Why had they all gathered at this unimposing burger stand? Why the subterfuge?

The reason was simple. Ever since the fiasco at Appalachin, when the law had swooped down and netted a haul of leading racketeers, the organization had gone to extremes trying to come up with secret hiding places for its annual convention. Four years before, the Dons had all donned (a forgiveable pun) scuba outfits and held their conclave at the bottom of Sea World in San Diego, but it had been hard to conduct the routine business with dolphins and barracudas nipping at their airhoses. Three years ago, operating under the theory that the best place to hide a tree is in a forest, they had all disguised themselves as pine trees in a lonely section outside Quebec, but once again the meeting had been disrupted, this time by drunken, axe-wielding Canadian loggers, who, before they could be halted, had sent three Dons floating down the river on the way to the paper mill, where all ended up not only on the front page of the Detroit *Free Press*, but as the front page of the Detroit *Free Press*. They'd gotten a break two years ago by deciding to stage the parley at a Chicago moviehouse screening "Myra Breckinridge," and this location had proved an excellent place to discuss Family affairs, for not only was the theater empty but even the projectionist had not bothered to show up. But last year's choice had been an unmitigated catastrophe. Someone had suggested assembling in an ambience where they could blend in and hardly be distinguishable from the other shady individuals, but because of the noise and confusion they had vowed never again to attend the Democratic National Convention.

Thus, the skullduggery that had led them to Paramus.

In order to maintain the fiction of a smoothly functioning MacDonaldi operation, the Dons were deployed at various stations behind the stainless steel counter. The host, Don MacDonaldi, known to his peers as the Franchising Don, stood at the squidburger section, knowing from past sales experience he would get little action and thus be able to keep an eye on his peers. Behind the grill, spatula in one hand, five knobby fingers of the other within easy reach of the Beretta in his hip holster, was Don Rickeleoni, the Insulting Don, the kingpin of the Las Vegas territory, owner of the Nina, the Pinta and the Santa Maria, the three foremost gambling casinos and hotels on the Strip. Watching a large burger disintegrating into the size of a dime as the heat of the grill eroded what few nutrients it held, the bald, hatchetfaced Rickeleoni snapped, "Some hamburger. I've seen more meat on a flea's knee." When MacDonaldi looked up with some asperity, he grinned. "You restaurant owners never laugh. Just sit there and wait for the broccoli to rot." He took another look at the diminishing patty. "If you don't get better meat, you'll be back in your old job where I found you, squeezing olives and molesting zucchini." Jokingly he said to the other Dons, "Is he moving toward me? But we have fun, right, gang? After all, we're all together in this enterprise, aren't we? I, the boss of Vegas, and you a restaurant owner who has brought his tasty product to the mouths of millions of people. And I say this from the bottom of my heart. I never liked you, MacDonaldi. Why don't you go back to your fifty-room estate and watch your Japanese gardener attack your wife on December 7th?"

Grinning at Rickeleoni's scattershot monologue was the skinny Don Knottso, the Nervous Don, head of the New England Family, who had made his millions controlling the massage parlor industries, a man who could not only rub you in, but, if the occasion demanded, rub you out. He had been put at the French fries station so that his quivering hands could shake the wire net, allowing the excess oil to drain off. At the soft ice cream machine was the tall, bronzed Don Comello, the Singing Don of the Midwest, a man who had an iron grasp upon the jukebox trade and who had some pretensions as a crooner. He had packed his thousands of jukeboxes with his own recording of "There's Lead in My Bed, 'Cause Tm All Shot Up Over You" and placed his armed goons by every machine to ensure that his was the only platter played. Despite this blatant intimidation, 50,000 people gladly gave up their lives for the cause of good music, and he finally abandoned his career. Watching the chocolate and vanilla go plop-plop-plop, he became strangely sentimental and broke into a song once used by those in the extortion rackets, a haunting lyric to the tune of "Come Back to Sorrento."

If you guys don't pay your rent-o,
We will stick you in cement-o
Ship you back to old Sorrento,
With an icepick in your ear.

"Bravo, bravo!" The compliment burst from the throat of Don Cherri, the Golfing Don, not a bad little singer himself. Cherri was the capo of the Deep South, who controlled bordellos, vibrator factories, porno publishing houses. It was said, though never proved, that he was still selling slaves to Mississippi plantation owners.

"Aha," said Mac Donaldi. "Our wise old *compadre* has appeared. Let the meeting begin."

Into the establishment waddled the *shtarker foon alle di shtarkeronis*, the boss of bosses, Don Guido Provolone. Behind him trailed his entourage, his sons, Fungi, Carmine and Nicholas, and the *calculatori*. His face, swollen with six boxfuls of Kleenex for if it ever had to appear imposing now was the time, earned their instant respect. He took his position as head counterman.

"My fellows," he spoke in his hoarse voice, "let us begin by expressing our deep gratitude to Don MacDonaldi for offering his magnificent roadside palazzo to us as a meeting place."

"Here! Here!" the Dons roared, except for Rickeleoni, who cried, "This place has all the charm of a drunk tank."

A withering glance from Don Provolone ended what could have been the jumping off one-liner for a forty-five minute lounge act.

"Let us take up Numero Uno on the agenda." Don Provolone unfolded a paper.

"What's that mean?" asked Don Knottso timidly.

"Dummy, dummy, dummy!" screamed Don Rickeleoni. "That means Number One. That's the last time we hire a Don from Kelly Girls."

"Outside is a man who wishes to make a proposal to us."

"Let him enter," said Don MacDonaldi.

Bouncing into the room on his Nunn Bush executive specials came a distinguished-looking man in a Bill Blass suit, striped shirt with cufflinks in the likeness of Commander Whitehead, a wide paisley tie, and a gray walrus moustache which twitched excitedly as he went into his spiel.

"Gentlemen, I'm Winston J. Cubberly, promotional director of Batton, Barton, Bitten & Rabid, the Madison Avenue Advertising Agency, and my team at the shop has put together an absolutely, can't-be-topped program of public relations for your organization."

"We ain't too crazy about publicity... no offense, Mister," grunted Don Comello.

"But, gentlemen, we at BBB&R think you're missing the boat..."

"Missing the boat is very desirable in our business," Don Provolone interrupted. "But we will hear you out."

Cubberly opened an attaché case and six Dons went for their sidearms in unison. "Fellows, here are some undeniable facts. You are beyond question the biggest single industry in the country, perhaps the world. Your combined holdings dwarf U.S. Steel, Chrysler, Xerox. If Ford knew what you were doing, believe me, they'd have a better idea. When you infiltrated and took over the entire restaurant business, Alka Seltzer couldn't believe that you ate the whole thing. Let's face it. You're big business and as such you should be represented by a dignified advertising campaign that sells your goods in the marketplace and proffers an acceptable image to the public. You've got to scrap that old sinister Warner Brothers look, those terrible black suits and yellow ties, those bulletproof limos. It's just old fedora. It isn't being done anymore."

"What do you propose we should become?" Don Provolone said wryly.

"Well, this is just off the top of my Head & Shoulders, if you'll pardon a little Mad Ave client pun, but to begin with you should all be completely restyled, you know, some kicky shirts and Levi's hopsack flares. You know how the public loves to see its captains of commerce lolling about in leisure wear. You, Don Provolone, you're a natural for a big spread in Fortune Mag, the little woman over her Hotpoint turning out a batch of lasagna... your sons playing touch football, throwing the long bomb "

At the word "bomb" six hands again flew toward their pieces.

"You fellows should be tooling around in a perky little Dodger Swinger. We'd arrange for you to have some really chic offices instead conducting your business in deserted warehouses... oh, just a ton of tasty touches I haven't even gotten into. Of course, all this represents a drastic break with tradition, as we 'Future Shock' boys understand, but let's give it a chance. Let's drop it on the Teflon and see if it sticks. Or, to use your own patois, let's work it over in the alley and see if it bleeds."

"Let's do that," Don Provolone agreed. He crooked a finger and six weapons roared as one. "Fungi," he barked, "take Mr. Cubberly outside, and carefully, so he shouldn't slop up the welcome mat. Now for Item Two on the agenda. Don Cherri has requested an audience."

"Fellow Dons," the Southland's boss began, "I'm having a problem with the hookers in my joints. Ever since this Women's Lib crap started, they're demanding more money, night-care centers, the right to choose their own clientele, all that militant garbage. And this could be veryexpensive. Just to change all their calling cards from 'Miss' to 'Ms.' could cost me a small fortune in printing."

"I have an answer," Don Provolone said. "The next time one of these ultra-militants threatens to bum her bra, we'll make sure she's.wearing it at the time. That should settle that."

At that moment a teen-aged couple walked into MacDonaldi's, sending each of the Dons scurrying to his appointed station.

Don Provolone, pencil hovering over his notebook, said, "What would you like?"

"Two milk shakes," the boy said.

"What flavor?" the Don said to the girl.

"Pineapple."

"Two pineapples!" the Don shouted and suddenly his fellow Dons were diving under the steam tables, their guns out again.

"No, no, not pineapples. *Pineapples*." the Don told his terrified brethren.

Mollified, the other Dons rose, filled the order, and sent the couple on their way.

"What is this last item, captioned PB, on the agenda?" said a curious Don MacDonaldi.

"That, my fellow overlords, is a matter which concerns me personally," Don Provolone said. The others left their stations and walked to his side, for when Guido Provolone brought up an item, it required their closest attention.

"PB is the code for Peanut Brittle."

There was an excited chattering among the other five. Don Provolone picked up one of MacDonaldi's double burgers and rapped it on the steel counter for attention, putting a deep dent in the counter. "I see you are combining your cement business with your burger business," he commented. Then he continued. "A few days ago I was in my garden pruning my new *ruthi buzzi* azalea when a little maid in the garb of a Fireside Girl knocked at my gate."

"What is a Fireside Girl?" asked Don Comello.

"This is an organization of young ladies who wear a kind of scouting uniform and perform deeds of charity financed in the main by the sale of boxes of peanut brittle such as this..." He took out of the *calculatori's* briefcase a carton and dumped its contents on a table. "This substance sells for one dollar a box."

"So?" This from Don MacDonaldi.

"The child from whom I purchased the candy informed me that yearly her organization sells 200 million boxes. At a dollar a throw, this is nothing to be sneezed at." And if it were, the Don thought, what could I do? All my Kleenex is in my mouth. "*Compadres*, I propose to take over this peanut brittle industry."

"Good," Don Cherri said. "And you, of course, will share this bounteous windfall with our Families on the usual fifty-fifty basis."

"No."

Although spoken softly, the word reverberated like a cannon shot. Don Provolone, the Godfather, had said no. Though they masked their faces with casual unconcern, the Don could sense the smoldering resentment among his fellow balebatim.

"My friends, I am reaching the age where my body is crying for a slowdown. My Contadina wishes me to spend more time with my sons, aiding them in the development of their characters."

From the comer of the room came the thumping of the Spaulding and, "My name is Carmine... and my wife's name is Carlotta... we come from Covington... and we sell cocaine..."

"As you can see, Carmine especially needs my fatherly guidance. I am sixty years old now and I tire of strife, scheming and bloodshed. By taking over this new source of revenue I will be assured that my Family will be well provided for in the days when I am basking in my retirement development, Sun City, Sicily. My *calculatori* informs me that it will cost me nine cents to produce the box and the candy, perhaps even ten cents if there is to be peanuts in the brittle. Add another nine cents per box for the Fireside Girls for distribution, another penny a box for the contract that will dispose of the present factory owners, and that leaves eighty cents a box clear profit for the Provolone Family."

"One hundred sixty million dollars per annum," said the *calculatori*.

"One hundred sixty million dollars a year and we are not to get our taste at the trough?" Don Cherri's voice was mild, but with hardness not far from the surface.

"Come, let us reason together," urged Don Provolone. For some unaccountable reason these words came out not in his own dialect, but in the twang of a Johnson City, Texas, politician, an oddity which only occurred when he made this statement. When he did, he would fondly refer to his Family as "Contadina Bird," "Fungi Bird," etc. and be possessed of a terrible need to display his appendicitis scar. "You all have pies in which I have no finger. Why can I not have a pie of my own?"

"We do not mind a pie," said Don Rickeleoni, "but you've just put the whole bakery in your name. Is this to be your final decision?"

"Si," Don Provolone said.

" 'Si?' What does that mean?" asked Don Knottso.

"Dummy, dummy, dummy!" shrieked Rickeleoni again. "Why don't you go back to Vermont, sit under a sugar maple and suck sap?"

"Very well," said Don MacDonaldi. "If this is your decision..." He left the sentence unfinished but there was a stiffness in the way he walked out that had nothing to do with the cardboard he had forgotten to remove from his Fruit of the Loom shorts. The other Dons, their mouths taut and twisted, shook his hand briskly and also departed. Soon the lot was booming with the ignition of V-8 engines and then they were gone their separate ways.

"What do you think of the reception accorded my proposal, my sons?"

"Geez, Poppa," said Fungi. "We been here so long. I got a broad waitin' for me on the West Side, greatest set of *knockerinos* you ever saw. Can't we go home now?"

"And you, Carmine?"

The rubber ball thumped once more. "My name is Carmine... and my wife's..."

The Don wearily held up his hand. "You, Nicholas?"

"Poppa, these men are incensed." Nicholas bowed his cello, the lovely notes of DeBakey's "Afternoon of a Transplant" issuing from the supple strings. "They will not take this lying down."

"That's what this chick is doing on the West Side right now—lying down. And I'm wastin' my time in this hamburger joint," Fungi said with some irritation.

"And you, *calculatori?*"

The tiny Pinsky worked his fingers over his ever present IBM tabulator. "My calculations show odds of 400 to 1 in favor of treachery and war."

A dark frown on his face, Don Provolone walked into the New Jersey night. Before he reached his car he heard a groan and then saw the blood-stained Cubberly propped up against the trunk.

"Fellas, I hate to be a drag," the ad man said, "but if any of you are going near a hospital, I sure as hell would appreciate a lift. And listen, my proposal is not chiseled in granite. God knows, we can always make modifications. You don't have to drive a Dodge Swinger. It could be a Torino; that's more in keeping with your ethnic feel, isn't it? And if you don't like Levi's..."

They pushed him to the asphalt and drove off.

CHAPTER FIVE

"Fasten your seat belt, please," chirped Terri Tinytush, the winsome, sparkling-eyed stewardess in first class on Worldways Air Lines Flight 760 from New York to Los Angeles. As she undulated down the wide aisle checking each passenger's belt, Lazar Pinsky caught a generous view of her long stems and the firm, compact buttocks they supported. The hell with Continental Airlines, he thought. Here is the "proud bird with the golden tail."

Below, shimmering in the heat of midday, was the vast whiteness of this land of dreams. Now the 747 was banking over Beverly Hills. Looking down he could see the rich people on their capacious green lawns, watering the poor people. The giant freeways, their arteries clogged as usual, looked like a cardiogram in Dr. Barnard's treatment room. Flight 760 had been fairly uneventful, save for a few insignificant, hardly-worth-bothering-about incidents. The Polish hijacker's demands had been met by a cool Worldways administrator, who recently had been appointed vice president in charge of hijackings. The man had been given $500,000 and a map and then had jumped out over Hamtramck, Michigan, but in the excitement he had forgotten his parachute. True, he had not lived to enjoy his purloined money, but Casmir Predpelski would go down in the Guinness Book as the holder of the world's record for freefalling. The Cuban hijacker had been shot to death in a bitter argument with the Algerian hijacker over two proposed landing places. The Algerian, in turn, had been karate-kicked to eternity by the dying Cuban, thus canceling out the threat.

With a fork Pinsky made a last desultory poke at the Macadamia nuts in front of his seat, sending a man named Morton Macadamia running down the aisle toward the lavatory, clutching his pain-racked genitalia. The little *calculatori*'s face was wrinkled with worry. He had pleaded not to be sent to the coast at this ominous time, aware of the mounting dangers that faced his Don in his absence, but loyal servant that he was, he had reluctantly consented to the errand. He could not do less for the great Don who had lifted him from the streets of the Bronx and given him such eminence.

In 1933, the heart of the Great Depression, in the Jewish ghetto of the East Bronx, Sara and Moses Pinsky, his parents, unable to pay the rent on their roach-ridden railroad flat, had been forced to live on the fire escape. Six months of this horrific way of life had taken their toll. They had died of rust, leaving little Lazar a penniless orphan. The bright tot, forced to fend for himself, made his way to the area's marketplace, Jennings Street, and there slept in rent-free, malodorous herring barrels.

During these parlous times the housewives would come to the market, drawn by the Yiddish cries of merchants hawking their wares. Little Lazar would wait for a vendor to sell a woman a herring, sever the head, and wrap the balance of the evening meal in the lady's copy of the *Jewish Daily Forward*. He existed on these discarded fish-heads for many a month and during the biting winters when no fish-heads were available would eat the *Jewish Daily Forward*.

His body thus crammed with ancient Jewish wisdom, from the Letters to the Editor columns in his intestines to the stories of Sholem Aleichem in his pancreas, Lazar, despite the dismal poverty of his life, became the most outstanding student in P.S. 61, time and time again topping the honors list in mathematics. Because of the marine essence that had so worked itself into his ragged clothing, stringy hair and pores, Lazar was generally shunned by his schoolmates and teachers. On graduation day while the rest of the class received its diplomas in the auditorium, Lazar got his parchment in the boathouse of the lake in Crotona Park... from the end of a long stick held by an assistant principal.

In 1934, while conducting a protective reaction strike at Ishkowitz's fancy fruit and vegetable store on Bathgate Avenue, which culminated in the dynamiting of Mr. Ishkowitz, Don Provolone was touched by the figure of the ragged urchin sitting on the corner chewing on a ball of tinfoil garnered from 300 packs of Wings, and reciting logarithms at breathtaking speed. Sensing that this child had a gift that would prove invaluable to his then growing organization, Don Provolone gave the lad a wad of fifty-dollar bills (which he almost ate, under the mistaken impression they were soup greens), a position as a top numbers banker in Harlem, and to make him more acceptable to the general public, a season's ticket to the Luxor Baths. From that day on he had been raised almost as a son by the man he grew to love and honor as the Godfather. Though he had been made aware he could never inherit the crown because of his nonclan birth, nevertheless in years to come he would rise to the position of the *calculatori*, a man whose judgment was always sought.

The thump of the jet's tires on the tarmac jarred Pinsky out of his memories and also jarred the nuts of Macadamia, who had not returned to his seat belt in time, sending Morton howling back to the lavatory, this time a soprano. The silver bird taxied to its boarding tunnel and was hooked on. In an hour Pinsky was at the entrance of the Dizzy Studios, the gateway to which was the mouth of Dizzy Duck.

Passing through Dizzy's quacking bill automatically started a tape recording of the Dizzyland choir.

> *Welcome, welcome, young and old,*
> *To the land where tales are told,*
> *Of knights and fairy queens so grand,*
> *You've just stepped in Dizzyland.*

And something else, the *calculatori's* nose broadcast, as he scraped a clot of some foul substance from the heel of his right shoe. But in a studio whose stars were frequently furry little friends of the forest, this was to be expected. For all he knew, he had trampled upon the excrement of an Oscar winner.

Now the choir was singing the jolly, toe-tapping anthem.

Who's the funny little guy,
Who always makes us gay?
He's our pal... D-I-Z-Z...
Y D-U-C-K!

The receptionist felt a chill in the presence of the hard-eyed little man in the black suit and yellow tie who stood before her desk. There was the smell of danger and menace swirling about his figure, and also a slight whiff of herring—the *calculatori* had never been quite able to expunge the scent of his past, several thousand crates of Dial soap to the contrary. How different he was from the tall, blond, open-faced animators, story artists and cameramen who comprised the lighthearted family of Wally Dizzy. She motioned, "This way please, Mr. Pinsky," and he followed her clicking heels to a door whose knocker was the head of the lovable Dizzy Duck.

Behind an untidy pile of scripts, storyboards and set designs was the great one himself, Wally Dizzy, a lean, rugged man in a touristy Hawaiian shirt whose multihued blossoms ran rampantly, canary-yellow slacks, and white loafers. His Crest-polished teeth closed around a pipe, sending puffs of Carter Hall tobacco throughout the room.

The chicks are back, thought Pinsky, who reached for Dizzy's hand and got a clearly unfriendly clasp. Dizzy, unconsciously sensing he had touched a source of botulism, pulled back his hand and wiped it with a checkered gingham handkerchief. Then he got down to business. This unpleasant little emissary from sinful New York would have to be dealt with summarily.

"I'm a busy man, Mr. Pinsky, with a lot to do today. I have agreed to see you because Morrie Murray, the head of the Morrie Murray agency with whom I often do business [and which my Don owns, thought the *calculatori*] suggested I grant you an appointment."

"I appreciate the honor of being here, the birthplace of so many of my own childish fantasies, Mr. Dizzy. I will come to the point. My client and dear friend has a godson, the eminent singer, Engelbrute Pumpernickel."

"The eminent, off-key greaseball, womanizer and drinker of cheap wine you mean, Mr. Pinsky. I know why you are here—I also have my spies. The answer is no. I would not besmirch a picture as lovely as 'The Nun That Kicked a Computer' by presenting the X-rated face of a gang-connected wastrel like Mr. Pumpernickel. I know who your 'client and dear friend' is, Mr. Pinsky, the infamous Guido Provolone. Wally Dizzy did not build an empire by dillydallying and shillyshallying... or even by dillyshallying and shillydallying, although once in my impetuous youth I did willy wonka. Again I say no."

"Please do not make such a precipitate decision, Mr. Dizzy. Sleep on it, won't you? I will be in town for a few days at the Beverly Hiltoni Hotel."

"My mind is made up, Mr. Pinsky. But since you have traveled so far, can I not show you the fruits of my labor, my kingdom of decency, before you return to your dirty world of crime and degradation? Come, let me take you on a personal tour of Dizzy Studios."

The *calculatori* said yes and tagged after the robust Dizzy into a hallway. "Here," Dizzy indicated with pride, "is the soundstage where we are filming The Nun.'" Pinsky was amazed: in this cavernous room they had re-created the shrine of Lourdes, the main laboratory at IBM, and for some unfathomable reason, an Earl Scheib $29.95 auto paint shop. In a comer rehearsing her song, "The Halls Are Alive With the Sound of Muzak," was the sweet-faced starlet, Gloria Goody, who had won the coveted role of Sister Cherubica after beating out the lovely Doreen Daylight in a face-to-face competition—a freckle-off, besting Miss Daylight by 54,110 freckles to 54,108. But Gloria, already schooled in the unscrupulous ways of Hollywood, had not told the judges that her two-freckle margin was in actuality a mole and a liver spot. Lifting her cowl, she aimed her adorable, snub-nosed face at the bandleader and said icily, "Who's the motherfucker who hit that klinker in the bridge?"

Wally Dizzy choked a bit, then smiled. "Gloria has an unfortunate penchant for street vulgarity at times, gained, no doubt, from her formative years as a truck-stop waitress in Barstow."

Quitting the soundstage, they walked into the recording room where Mel Blink, the famed voice of Dizzy Duck, was quacking merrily away in synchronization to the film strip on the movieola. "Hi, Mel," Dizzy said. Mel cheerily waved a webbed hand and went on quacking. "He's been doing Dizzy for twenty-five years," the creator explained, "and a complete process of self-identification has set in. Other stars go to Palm Springs for the weekend. Mel hangs around marshes and bites hunters."

"And here," beamed Wally Dizzy with fatherly pride, "is the little feller that started the whole thing."

In a small anteroom, where organ music continually played the anthem to Dizzy heard at the gate, Wally Dizzy fell to his knees and lit a small votive candle. There on a yellowed storyboard was the original drawing of Dizzy Duck with the letters "by Wally Dizzy, 1931" scrawled beneath.

"I was just a kid in Muncie, Indiana, working for the Muncie *Times-Journal-Gazette-Clarion* as copyboy, go-fer, and coffeemaker when the editor noticed the little sketches I had left on his desk. He was so thrilled by the little quacker that the very next week my first Dizzy Duck cartoon strip was running on page 38. Then the Fort Wayne Dispatch picked it up, Then the Wilkes-Barre Chronicle, and in a year I was syndicated in 154 papers. An old friend, Amos Pettibone, financed the first Dizzy Duck film cartoon. The rest is history. 'Course, old Dizzy's changed a bit since then. I got rid of the old middy blouse and cap after a while and today he's wearing his feathers longer, has a Day-Glo bill and tie-dyed feet. Here's the way he'll appear in his latest full-length cartoon, 'Dizzy Duck and Sundance Squirrel.' "

He fondled a newly inked figure of Dizzy on a large storyboard. "I myself do all the work on the little feller, never let another artist touch him. My 150 animators just concentrate on the background stuff. I fully expect his next film to gross sixty million dollars."

Pinsky made a few punches at his tabulator. "Seventy million, not counting the East Indies and Pitcairn Island."

"Hey, you're a bright fellow, Pinsky," Dizzy said, new respect on his granite features. "Why don't you leave this Provolone character and work for me?"

"I have sworn my loyalty to the Don. Is your decision on Mr. Pumpernickel final?"

"Irrevocable. Good day, Mr. Pinsky."

Walking through the gates toward his limousine, he knew the only course left was the Don's dictum: "I'll send him a sign he can't decline."

To the pair of burly men slouched in the car he whispered a few brief sentences, ending with the word "tonight."

"Jesus, I bane glad to get rid of him, yumpin' yiminy, by golly," muttered Captain Erik Cigar of the S.S. *Hooker*, a tramp steamer plying the Gulf of Dmitri Tiomkin. "Him" was the sullen, uncommunicative and terrifying passenger he had been carrying for three weeks since his ship docked at Sydney under sealed orders. Bonfiglio "The Butcher" Bucceroni had not actually disrupted the routine of the battered hulk, keeping to himself for the most part during the voyage, but the little things he did proved unsettling to even the crew of hardened old Lascars, the scum of the earth. Punching a hole in the main boiler with his fist had not endeared him to the "black gang" in the hold, nor had the sailors been pleased when one morning he ate the shuffleboard set, thinking it was Aunt Jemima pancakes, washing it down with a barrel of 30-weight crude oil.

But now the rendezvous point, a mile off Phuc Hu in South Cheong-Sam, a reputed hotbed of Ho Ho Ho's guerrilla insurgency, had been reached. As per instructions, there was the sampan bobbing in the chill, gray waters, CIA operative Neil McCormick at the tiller. Although the secret agent wore the quilted coat and black pajamas of the countryside and had put on a wig to hide his sandy crewcut, his necktie, flashing its "America, Love It or Leave

It" message had compromised his disguise somewhat, Captain Cigar shrewdly reasoned.

"The Butcher," disdaining the use of a rope ladder, kicked a gaping hole in the ship's railing and dived over the side, striking the bottom of the sampan headfirst. The blow proved grievous to the sampan, which began filling up with the murky water.

"The village is crawling with Ho people, according to this morning's recon flyover and Form 8788-Intell report. There may be some friendly gooks in there, so be as selective as you can," McCormick said.

When they came in sight of the beach, McCormick doused his cigarette and made what ultimately proved to be a rather foolish statement. "Well, I'm the only one who knows what you're here for, Mr. Bucceroni, so..."

Just then, at 0600 hours, the sampan hit the sand bar. At 0601, Bucceroni, following the instincts of a lifetime, made sure of his personal security by dealing CIA operative McCormick and his sampan a blow that sent both to the bottom.

At 0603 hours he strode into the collection of thatched huts and cooking fires that was Phuc Hu.

"Greetings," smiled a toothless old-timer, inhaling his morning opium. "I am Nguyen Nu Nu, the headman of this village. May I help you, oh brawny, round-eyed visitor?"

"Where are the guerrillas?" grunted "The Butcher."

Shrugging, the headman said, "Who can tell? They are like lightning bugs, here one moment, gone the next."

Puzzled by the sameness of the yellow faces curiously peering into his, "The Butcher" made a snap decision to drop any notion of selectivity, uprooted a banyan tree and used it like a mighty club to send the elder and all his charges to their ancestors via special-delivery airmail. Satisfied that there was nothing alive, he moved on to the next village.

At 6 A.M. the Dizzy Duck watch on his creator's left wrist quacked six times, rousing Wally Dizzy from his usual G-rated dream of jolly, rotund little munchkins, scrappy woodpeckers, giggling rabbits and golden-haired children standing in long lines around theaters displaying his motion pictures. His wife, Wilma, as usual, slept in her opulent bedroom on the far side of the estate, since the Dizzys from the outset of their marriage forty years ago had made a solemn promise never to mar their relationship by doing *that*.

Half awake, he mulled over the visitation of this Pinsky fellow, chuckling at the very notion that the cold-eyed little ferret and his "client" in the East could induce a titan like himself to betray those golden-haired children by putting into one of his films this unheroic, swarthy saloon rake.

Perhaps those effete snobs of Eastern critics had termed his actors "plastic," but, by Jove, at least they were red, white, and true-blue American plastic and there was no room in the wonderful world of Dizzy for such plug-uglies like Engelbrute Pumpernickel.

Then Wally Dizzy noticed something strange. The adorable chickadees and chipmunks who were on a $300-a-week retainer to romp outside his bedroom window filling his wakeup moments with bucolic sounds were silent. "Sing, you little creeps!" he shouted, but the silence held. And what had happened to the babbling brook, which was on an even bigger retainer? It was not babbling over the smooth stones. What was going on here? A mutiny in fantasyland? An insurrection? He bit his tongue. "Insurrection" was a highly inappropriate word in his lexicon, far too close to hardcore pornography.

Something familiar caused his nostrils to twitch. He inhaled deeply to verify his guess. India ink, the liquid he had turned into black gold all those years at the drawing board. But where was it coming from? He shifted his body and felt a wetness under his feet and around the cuffs of his pajamas and bedsocks.

He threw the blanket off with a sweep of his hand. My God, my God... India ink, running like a river gone mad! And at that instant Wally Dizzy knew that something evil had defiled his gingerbread and cinnamon world. He leaped from under the canopy of his four-poster and looked at the horrible trail of India ink leading to the foot of the bed.

He began to scream and scream and scream, trying to avert his eyes from the monstrosity before them, but unable to.

Splayed out on the soggy sheet was Dizzy Duck, or what remained of him. My God, they had ripped him from his storyboard, probably in midquack... callously ignoring the pulsating fountains of black ink pouring out of his torn body. The merry little eyes that Dizzy had sketched in with his Number Four Speedball pen only last night, eyes that had taken him a lifetime to develop, just the right blend of rascality and adorableness... and now they were bulging with horror. My God, how the "little fella" must have suffered! The fiends, for surely it had taken more than one to wrest the struggling duck from the paper, had not been content with just mutilating the eyes. From a slashed webbed foot gushed another revolting curlicue of India ink... feathers had been sliced from the duck's back... his rubbery bill, which had evoked laughter from millions each time it had twisted into an exasperated howl, had been crumpled like a fender in a nine-car collision and from it gurgled more tides of India ink. My God, my God, Dizzy shuddered. How much more ink could Dizzy bleed?

How in the name of Smucker's jelly and Jane Parker apple pie could he ever draw Dizzy Duck again after witnessing this mind-boggling evisceration performed upon his "child"?

In his mind he could hear the voice of Pinsky, "Is this your final decision?" And he knew what had prompted the assault. He, Wally Dizzy, king of an empire, had met his master in this malevolent gangster from New York and had been brought to his knees. If this Provolone could so brutalize Dizzy Duck, who would be next? Obviously these men would stop at nothing to achieve their aim. And then Wally Dizzy knew what he must do.

By RON A BORAX

HOLLYWOOD—Handsome Welsh singing star Engelbrute Pumpernickel today was given the plum role of Hermes the Shepherd Boy in Wally Dizzy's new multi-million-dollar film, "The Nun That Kicked a Computer," according to studio boss Dizzy. He replaces Sir John Laurence-Greengrave who withdrew from the part at the behest of the studio. "Sir John's a fine actor," Dizzy stated, "but lacks the stature to portray this complicated and many-faceted character. Anyway, I've always wanted to do a picture with Engelbrute, a great guy, a warm human being and the personification of all that has made the American dream."

Contacted at his home, Sir John expressed bitterness at being dropped by the Dizzy organization. "A man who has played 'Hamlet' for the Old Vic should have no problem hitting some goddam sheep with a stick."

Dizzy also announced cancellation of the scheduled full-length cartoon, "Dizzy Duck and Sundance Squirrel."

"I'm going to retire him because I feel America has come of age and is ready for more relevance than old Dizzy Duck can supply. Let him spend his golden years quacking off."

With a sigh of satisfaction Don Provolone put down the paper. "I am pleased, *calculatori*. Things appear to be going well, for my godson in Hollywood, for our new peanut brittle industry...

"The factories are humming, thanks to our new policy of having our shop stewards casually ambling about the assembly line carrying bazookas, and Provolone's Peanut Brittle is selling almost a million boxes a day," Pinsky informed the Don. "And our plan to send Fireside Girls into motels with tape recorders and Polaroid cameras has certainly sold more peanut brittle to nervous men in jockey shorts than we imagined."

Shoving his midday Kleenex into his mouth, the Don said, "And yet things are too quiet. I cannot believe the other Dons are letting this go unchallenged. But now this old body craves a sweet. I shall go down to Tootsie Rolli's candy shop."

"But you can't go alone, Godfather."

"Nonsense, Lazar, if I cannot walk in my own bailiwick without fear, then where can I go? If it pleases you, I shall have one of the boys accompany me."

Downstairs he saw Fungi on the phone, a noticeable bulge at his hip that was not a .45. "Baby," Fungi was saying, his eyes apop with desire, "I'll be over in ten minutes. Keep the Budweiser cold and your ass warm, *cara mia*."

No, Fungi did not appear amenable to an afternoon walk... a jump, perhaps, but not a walk. "Carmine?"

His second son stood in the yard, thumping his pink Spaulding high into the sun-splashed sky. "My name is Carmine... and my wife's name is Claudia... we come from Cleveland... and we sell cantaloupe..."

Why interrupt the lad's spirited fun? the Don thought. "Bounce away to your heart's content, my child," and he resnapped the trapdoor on Carmine's nighty-nights. "Where is Nicholas?" he asked of Contadina, who sat knitting a bulletproof jacket for the Don she hoped would be ready in time for the holidays.

"He is having lunch with the reed section of the New York Philharmonic. At his impressionable age he, alas, surrounds himself with bad companions "

"No matter, I shall go myself." Don Provolone slipped into an old mackinaw he had once worn in his youth on the icetruck during the Tong Wars of the late twenties. To look at him, one would never have believed this elderly man picking his way down the sidewalk, nodding at the old women in black shawls, commanded a fiefdom and the fierce loyalty of thousands.

"Hello, Godfather," said old Guiseppe Barberi, the haircutting bookie who had placed many a hot towel on the Don's face and a hot tip in his ear. He waved his razor cheerily in salute, inadvertently lopping off the head of Khartoum, the swaybacked horse of the old junk-dealer, Ragsi

Scavenged. Now he was shaking, hands with old Ricotta, the dairyman, and old Tony Kemtoni, the paint dealer, and old Giorgio Jesseloni, the neighborhood philosopher, who warmed the Don's heart with one of his typical verses:

Old friends are gold,
Who bring their rewards,
But what old friends need,
Is a couple young broads.

To repay Jesseloni for his sagacious thought, the Don reached into his mackinaw and gave the old savant 200 shares of a trucking company in Newark.

Tootsi Rolli's sweetshop had not changed in the fifty years it had been on the corner, the same marble counter and its neat little stools, the same swirled-metal ice-cream-parlor chairs, the same dead bluebottle flies in the windows. Rolli, an octogenarian who still voted for FDR and Fiorello La Guardia in each election, tottered to the front. "An honor to serve you, Don Provolone. Your sweet tooth nags again, eh? Will it be a Heide's banana, wax lips, Mary Jane... or perhaps some of your very own peanut brittle which this lovely child is waiting to sell to me."

The Don glanced at the other person in the shop and rejoiced to see that she was one of his very own Fireside Girls, attractively dressed in her little green uniform with merit badges on her chest... and an ample chest at that, he marveled. Ah, what wonders One-A-Day vitamins was doing for this generation, he noticed appreciatively.

Had not he been so concerned with his ravenous desire for sweets he might have noticed a few other discrepancies in her physique: her 5' 8" height, the powerful swell of her thighs, her rounded buttocks, and the dark roots lurking under her blonde sausage-curls, all untypical of the usual twelve-year-old in this worthy organization.

"I've been waiting for you, oh Don," she said sweetly, "with a report on my peanut brittle sales."

"How charming," the Don smiled. "And where is your report?"

"Here." The report came from the Saturday night special she yanked from her peanut brittle box. Six times it crashed into his body and Don Guido Provolone, cursing himself for his laxity even as he fell, slumped over the book rack, his life's claret pouring over fan magazine covers headlining "ARI REFUSES TO BEAR MY CHILD, SEZ JACKIE," "WHAT CLIFFORD AND HELGA DIDN'T TELL LIZ AND RICHARD OR ANDY AND CLAUDINE ABOUT JANE'S TRIP TO HANOI."

Hurling the gun contemptuously onto the gasping face of the Don, the Fireside Girl stepped casually into the street and into a waiting orchid-colored Cadillac with a black man behind the wheel. The vehicle zipped down Mulberry Street and out of sight.

In a few minutes the word was all over the neighborhood, all over Manhattan and being pumped by frantic newsmen to the wire services and TV. Don Provolone, the boss of bosses, was dying.

CHAPTER SIX

The telephone burred in the Fifth Avenue apartment of Consuelo Motors, the imperious, jet-setting heiress to the automotive fortune of her father, General Jack Motors. At first she did not hear it, for it was smothered by the thunderous noise of the piston-rodlike device rammed deeply into her grotto of desire, a sound she had known only once before on the assembly line of Daddy's plant in Detroit, the globally famous Motors Motors, which employed 48,000 men to build the cars and 79,000 others in public relations whose main job was apologizing to the public for the slipshod work of the 48,000.

"Oh, Fungi, Fungi, Fungi!" she shrieked in ecstasy. "Oh, now I know what fuel injection really means!" She climaxed for the tenth time in as many minutes. Had her father been able to harness her sexual energies to one of his products, it would have conquered the Baja, unsalted the flats at Bonneville, and melted a set of radial tires.

"Oh, oh, oh," she moaned. Never had she known such fulfillment—not even in her publicized affairs with Sterling Musk, the British race driver, who did not confine his pitstops to the Indy 500... nor with Boris Passkey, the Russian champion of chess and sex, who had on his twenty-fifth move thrillingly blocked her nook with his rook... nor even with Poppa Jock, the mulatto dictator of the island of San Bimbo, considered one of the world's great Casanovas and a man who did strange things with iguanas—as she was experiencing with this insatiable animal of gangster origin.

"What is this 'oh, oh, oh' crap?" Fungi said angrily. "I'm only up to the foreplay."

Yielding regretfully to the insistent ring, she reached for the Princess phone on her night table. "It's for you, darling."

"What?" Fungi paled. "Pop's been shot? Momma mia, I'll be right over in "

Consuelo had a second thought and a third wind, and clasped his divine rod.

"In about an hour," Fungi said, returning to his work. "But tell him my thoughts are ever with him."

CHAPTER SEVEN

Fortunately, because it was Wednesday and also because it was the opening day of the Che Guevara Golf Classic at the nearby Swappingmate Country Club in Great Neck, Long Island, all the nation's leading surgeons were within a few miles of Mount Manischewitz Hospital where the Don lay in extremis, and a dozen of these duffers, still in their lime-colored slacks and cleated Foot-Joy shoes, were recruited by a fervent plea from Pinsky and the business end of .38 Mob Positive Specials held by Renzo and Nunzio. They leaped into their eight-cylinder, air conditioned, all-option golf carts and, led by the Family limousine, were at the Midtown Tunnel in twenty-five minutes; in another five, they were out of their Arnold Palmer golf gloves and into their Marcus Welby rubber gloves.

Only the faintest of breathing came from the perforated body. Small blips bleep-bleeped across the monitor linked to the Don's body in the intensive-care unit. An anxious young intern, his eyes riveted to the screen, called out excitedly, "Hey, there's a large blip. The old boy is gaining."

"No," said crusty old Head Nurse Nosey Parker, "that one means we're picking up a Russian submarine off Jones Beach. Probably in the Potemkin class from the size of the blip. I'm afraid this old man is on his way out."

"We can use one of two methods," said Dr. Otis Elevator, the prominent neurosurgeon who had reached the top in his field. "We can miniaturize a team of doctors to the size of paramecia, inject them into his veins and let them attack the bullets from his interior. I know it'll work. I saw it done on a rerun of 'Fantastic Voyage' last week."

"There's no time for that. I suggest using leeches, mandrake roots, hot poultices, and cupping," said Dr. Cotton Mather, the famed surgeon from Salem, Massachusetts, an odd sight in his conical cap and black cape with its drawings of crescents and stars.

"Or," Dr. Elevator said resignedly, "we can do it ourselves."

"Aw, golly," whimpered Dr. Clem McWhortey, the Galveston specialist. "An operation this difficult will strain my arms, maybe weaken my backswing, bring my slice back, hurt my short game. I don't know if I want to take that chance."

Nunzio prodded his ribs with the .38.

"But, on the other hand, I am sworn to the Hippocratic Oath," Dr. McWhortey said brightly. "Prepare the anesthesia."

Nunzio and Renzo dropped to their knees in the firing position.

"No fellas," the frightened surgeon said "Not Anastasia... *anesthesia.*"

The needle slid into the Don's vein. The eyelids rolled over the soft brown eyes and he was asleep. And as was customary, he knew this was an excellent opportunity to let his entire life flash before him.

The cold Polar wind whipped over the tundra and through the door of the tiny igloo. Nanookey of the North, the simple Eskimo woman, shrieked, for now her child was forcing his way through her womb and into the gelid world of the Arctic Circle.

"Muck-A-Luck!" she cried to her fur-wrapped husband, who sat over a hole in the ice with a fishing pole, munching Wrigley's blubbergum. "We have a man-child!"

At the sound of his wife's joyous news, Muck-A-Luck took his hand off the mammaries of the sea otter he had been caressing, for too long had he been deprived of Nanookey's womanhood. The otter looked at him reproachfully, its limpid eyes seeming to say, "You didn't tell me you were married."

"We shall call him Boogaloo of the Igloo, and he will grow to be a fearless hunter of lions and tigers and bears, oh my, lions and tigers and bears, oh my..."

On the operating table, the Don stirred and muttered something in his native tongue. Nunzio whispered to the doctors, "Do something quick! He's reliving the wrong life."

"It's a rather common occurrence," said Dr. Elevator. "Give him 2 ccs. of sodium sulfaborateem, and you'd better add a quart of Prestone antifreeze. He's shivering for some reason."

The needle slipped in again and the Don was back on the right memory track.

The sun-baked streets of Finobarbitoli, a sleepy village. The ever present dust. The squalor, the misery, everywhere the constant buzzing and nipping of those damned flies. Long before they had founded the infamous Black Hand Society to protect them against the avaricious landlords and corrupt *carabinieri*, the residents of this town had established the Black Flag Society to fend off the flies. And the famine, always the famine. How hard it was for Mother Nature's seeds to flourish in soil so unyielding and inhospitable. In the years between 1900 and 1910, only one gutsy radish was able to force its way into the sun, and the politicians had taken it. In later years, villagers who came to America would be amazed at the popularity of organic foods, for they had been eating lava all their lives in order to exist. And indeed, it was a *paesan'* who had allegedly invented the earliest formula for Preparation H, for when a man dined on volcanic rocks, he needed all the help he could get.

Such a life was not for young Guido Provolone. Many a night he sat by the light of a fire, dreaming of the Promised Land which lay beyond the sea, a land of milk and honey where swollen fruit hung from trees. Alas, all the ships to Israel were crowded, so as an alternative, he decided upon America, where reputedly gold lay in the streets and a man willing to toil hard could reap his reward.

Then the day he boarded the ship; people crowded like goats in stinking steerage, while goats, who were considered more valuable, lounged in deck chairs in first class and sipped Martinis.

And so young Guido left his homeland in the midst of the famine of 1914, arriving in America just in time for the hunger riots of 1915.

Immediately, he was met on the docks by two men in garish, checked suits, brown derbies and spats who through their rapid-fire conversation were able to con the young immigrant out of his meager savings in return for the deed to the Brooklyn Bridge. How his fellow immigrants had chortled at the young greenhorn's naiveté, but the day would come when Guido, at the height of his powers and with five hundred blacksuited, yellow-tied men behind him, would convince the city that the scrap of paper did indeed represent his ownership of the span and they would offer him no argument when he set up a bank of highly profitable toll booths.

Naturally, at the beginning he sought refuge in that crowded section of lower New York, where earlier arrivals had massed. He slept with twelve others in a single bed, where in a restless fit one night he rolled over and discovered Contadina Lombardo, a quiet, dark-eyed maid who already was working in a sweatshop drawing the unheard of salary of two dollars a week, plus all the perspiration she could carry home.

Love flickered between the two, there was a hasty marriage, and the young couple moved to another rooming house where they enjoyed the newfound privacy of a bed for six. Among those in that creaking bed had been Nunzio Fresca and Renzo Uncola, two men who would prove to be his lifelong associates. They had fled from Palermo for the simple crime of garroting twenty-seven men who had criticized their essay on nonviolence.

His dreams of wealth had faded in the harsh glare of reality. There was no gold in the streets and, in many sections, no streets in the streets. Now Guido was toiling eighteen hours a day with a pick and shovel hundreds of feet below the broiling city. He had already laid three miles of track when by chance he took a peek at the engineer's blueprints and told Mahoney, the Irish foreman, that this new means of transportation, this thing called the Third

Avenue El, should be built above the ground, not below it. Whereupon the opportunistic Mahoney had gone to the city fathers with a new concept, the "subway," which brought him fame and riches, but for Guido it only meant a reprimand and a sacking for failing to follow the engineer's plans.

Next he was hired by a Rumanian foreman, somewhat of an illiterate—for he also called himself Mahoney, for a construction job on 34th Street, but the Rumanian, instead of giving Guido one set of plans for a ten-story building and handing out the other nine sets to the various city departments concerned, gave them all to Guido. In vain, the young laborer tried to tell his overseer that a mistake had been made, but the language barrier proved insurmountable, since the Rumanian spoke only Urdu. Before anyone was aware of it, the energetic, eager-to-please Provolone had built ten ten-story buildings, one atop the other, until he had completed the Kong Building, tallest edifice in the world. The Rumanian, gulping at first at what he saw, slyly termed it a "skyscraper" and garnered accolades and wealth, while the exhausted Guido, who had spent nearly a year of his life on the project, was again chastised and dismissed for not following orders.

Although Guido had boosted his earnings to $6 a week—$4 of which the frugal Contadina used for rent, food and clothing, and $2 of which she squirreled away for a rainy day—he came to the sober conclusion that only by being his own boss could he achieve anything more than two dried sandwiches in a workman's pail.

Purchasing a horse, a wagon and a ton of ice, Guido roamed the streets of his neighborhood peddling his wares until one day he was accosted by two men in gaudy suits who grabbed the reins. "Gentlemen," he said politely, "I bought the Brooklyn Bridge from you years ago."

"Goombah," laughed one of the men. "Don't you recognize us? Maybe you would if we were lying on a bed watching you and Contadina consummate your marriage."

"Renzo! Nunzio!" Guido cried joyously and embraced his old bedmates and sex instructors. "How well you look."

"That's because we're not breaking our labonzas dragging blocks of ice around, you old stupido," Nunzio said. "We're making big money now working for Bofferoni, the white slaver. Come, let's have a drink at his place and maybe we can find something worth your while."

"But I can't leave my horse," Guido protested. Nunzio pulled out an imposing pistol and clapped it against the steed's head. It roared once. "You're out of business," he grinned. "Come with us."

"And to make sure..." Renzo added. He pulled out his own pistol and blasted away at the wagon until it was a heap of shavings and splinters. Guido was impressed. Here were his old friends in fine suits and elegant shoes. Truly, they had found the key to America's wealth and it was not by blood, sweat and hernias, a big money-making rock group he would one day control as the head of Knuckle Records.

"My God," said Dr. Elevator, his scalpel slicing into the bullet-ridden body, "with all this metal I'm pulling out, I'm not doing an operation; I'm doing a tune-up." He removed two more slugs and dropped them into the bloody bucket at his knee.

The chink of metal caused the Don to open one eye. "Could you hold the noise down, please? I'm getting to the good part of my life."

They injected another 2 ccs. of Sodium Sominex, he dropped back into his reverie, and they continued probing. "He's a tough old bird," mused Dr. McWhortey. "Luckily, there seems to be a sort of calcified layer around his vital organs that prevented the bullets from penetrating too deeply."

"I just ordered a biopsy on the stuff," Dr. Elevator revealed. "Those technicians at the lab must be boozing it up. They tell me it's Kleenex."

In the plush Chelsea section around 23rd Street, the horse carriages and newfangled motorcars of the rich parked in front of the glowing red lamps that lit the entrance to

Benvenuto Bofferoni's "Casa di Pussi," the house of the cats.

They walked through halls richly brocaded with flocking, not surprising, Guido thought, for flocking seemed to be the order of the day here at Bofferoni's. From locked rooms he could hear the jingle of coins, which denoted that a man was spending, and the squeaking of springs, which denoted the same thing.

In the anteroom, spread langorously on silken couches, were the heavily rouged, bold-eyed maidens. They greeted Nunzio and Renzo with cries of affection, but backed away disdainfully from the humble Guido, clutching his workman's cap. Bofferoni, a portly man whose gold teeth flashed as he lit a cigar with a dollar bill, said, "So this is your friend, the man who breaks his *labonza* working for the *corruptos*?" He laughed, patting Guido on the back. "Starting today you make thirty dollars a week in my service. A man such as I needs constant protection from my enemies. Do you swear your loyalty to me, Guido Provolone?"

"*Si*," Guido said.

"Then kneel and kiss my cigar."

Before he got to his feet, two buxom blondes rushed over to the newcomer and offered their favors. Guido, despite his loyalty to Contadina, was on the verge of accepting, for somehow he found the prospect of exchanging a piece of ice for a piece of ass suddenly enticing, but Nunzio held him back. "Get away," and he drove the girls off. "They have the *clapperia*, the sickness of the lower lips. They are not for you, good Guido." Guido, who had been looking around, started suddenly. Coming into the room were the venal Irish and Rumanian foremen who had climbed to glory on his back.

Now he would exact his revenge.

"Service them," he commanded the two blondes and felt a strange surge in his body. He, Guido Provolone, had tasted from the cup of power and it had been a sweet drink. For the first time in his life people quailed at a glance from his eyes. The two blondes grabbed his exploiters and led them into another room, where they would have momentary pleasure and terminal effects from a doseria.

His brain racing like a train on the subway he had built, Guido had an inspiration. "Some day, I would like to have a place like this, with money and power, and *soldati* to guard me."

Bofferoni laughed. "So the little immigrant who has only been here for a few seconds has big eyes for power. And when will you gain this power, oh *pipsqueakerini?*"

"Today. Now!" Guido swiftly said, pulling from his belt the last evidence of his former occupation, an icepick, and driving it home. Bofferoni, gasping more in disbelief than in pain, then in pain, for a man with a punctured heart had a heaven-sent right to gasp in pain, fell to the Persian rug. "But... but... you swore loyalty to me..."

"In this land of freedom, a man may change his mind, no?"

Bofferoni died that second.

Now there was a look of fear, even respect, on the faces of Nunzio and Renzo. What hidden fires burned in their little *compadre!* Truly, this man was bom to lead, and they would follow him the rest of their lives.

And so, with his first step onto the turnpike of treachery, Guido became ever emboldened, moving from bordello to gambling to extortion to Tinkers to Evers to Chance (for he now was involved in fixing sporting events), to bootlegging to hijacking to union domination to real estate—until he owned the Kong building he had made with his own hands, until he was the unquestioned king of crime, the *racketeer di racketeeroni*, the Godfather, Don Guido Provolone.

From now on everything he touched would turn to money. Indeed, one day in his garden while spading the soil to make a place for his long-stemmed garagiola, a type of gladiola that attracted flies but could not catch them, the Don hit an undiscovered pool of shiny liquid, which exploded into a gusher. He had struck olive oil and soon there would be a derrick and a thousand barrels a day.

The last flattened-out bullets clanged into the bucket. By now there was a three-foot pile of jagged metal, for the surgeons had not stopped at the removal of the six slugs pumped in by the Fireside Girl, but had taken out ten more from the gun of the notorious Dutch Cleanser, who had blasted the Don during the 1934 war; three from Scarface Scarlatti in Sheepshead Bay in 1935 during the Great Clam War; and a few dozen pieces of shrapnel from the movie, "Back to Bataan," when an overzealous John Wayne, who had destroyed all his enemies, had decided to hurl his last grenade into the audience at Loew's Sheridan.

Sixteen skilled hands sewed up the rent body, swabbed off the blood, and bandaged the wounds. The *calculatori's* IBM tabulator clicked away, providing a jolly counterpoint to the bleeping of the monitor. Click-bleep! Click-bleep! Click-bleep! "I now compute that the odds of my Don's recovery are 2.0067 to 1 in his favor. Gentlemen, you have done a masterful job. For your reward we will see to it that socialized medicine is cubbyholed in the next three sessions of Congress. Now, Renzo and Nunzio, let us take our Godfather home."

CHAPTER EIGHT

The Provolone Family, with the Don safely ensconced in an upstairs bedroom turned into a hospital ward, sat morosely at a table piled high with plates of Contadina's lasagna and 5,000 of her newly baked bullets, made from an ancient recipe of Leonardo DaVinci's.

The former was for the insides of the Family, the latter for the insides of the dogs who had gunned down their Godfather. *Soldati* were pouring in from every nook and cranny of the city, 250 from Nunzio's district in Brooklyn's Bensonhurst, another 180 from Renzo's Bronx territory. People from all over were coming in unasked: 28 from Howard Johnson's, 31 from Baskin-Robbins, 57 from Heinz, and from Parker 51.

In accordance with Fungi's orders, a huge, protective moat had been dug around the mansion, backing up traffic to 157th Street and causing the electrocution of ten Con Ed workers from exposed wires. But this was no time to be concerned with piddling side issues. The Great Peanut Brittle War was about to begin.

Carmine, visibly upset by the shooting, was mumbling, "C, my name is Carmine... and my wife's name is Lulubelle... we come from Kentucky... and we buy at a Safeway." Truly, Nicholas thought, my brother has become unhinged. Not only has he messed up his doggerel but he is bouncing his ball off-rhythm. The youngest son, who sat at the Stradivarius piano, the only one the famed maker of violins had ever carved, played a series of Beethoven's sonatas, which somehow all began to sound like "Take Me Out to the Ball Game." I, too, am upset, he noted.

Fungi, his temper at the boiling point, shouted, "Who dared to order the shooting of our Don? Rickeleoni, Knottso, Cherri... ?"

"Any or all of them," said the *calculatori*, "Your father and I knew they would not accept his total control of peanut brittle."

"The neighbors say the shooting was done by a Fireside Girl who was driven away by a colored one in a Cadillac," said Renzo chomping down on what he thought was Contadina's lasagna, but cringing as an exploding bullet flew from his teeth and killed one of the *soldati* from Bensonhurst. "See that the man's widow is royally treated."

The *calculatori's* tabulator clicked, he wrote out a check, including an extra 10 percent for combat pay, and slipped it into the pocket of the body being carried out.

"My informant, Fillipo the Fink, has not been sleeping," Nunzio said proudly. "We have now ascertained that Rocco the Rifle, Tulio the Trigger, and the girl whom he identified as Bonnie Barker, a hit girl..."

"A hit girl?" Fungi asked.

"Yes. Woman's Lib has opened many opportunities— and at equal pay," Nunzio said. "We have now ascertained that all three were free lances, not affiliated with any of the other Dons."

"Which is not to say they could not have been engaged by any of the other Dons," the *calculatori* said knowingly.

"Words, words, words," Fungi was impatient. "It's time for action. I say we go to the mattresses."

That night the war began in earnest. One of Don Rickeleoni's torpedoes, Ernest Chamberino, ran into Fungi's icepick while leaving the apartment of his paramour. In a few seconds Ernest obtained firsthand knowledge of the word *acupuncture*. A truckload of Nunzio's men burst into the jukebox warehouse of Don Comello on Tenth Avenue and not only left sixteen men dead, but as an added fillip replaced all of Don's records with those of Snooky Lanson. At midnight a handful of Renzo's goons hurled six plastique explosives into the hotel of visiting film director Frederico Antonionionioni, who actually had had nothing whatsoever to do with the attempted assassination, but a man with a sorry history of foisting terrible films upon the public certainly deserved a few bombs in return.

The next day truckloads of mattresses were unloaded in apartment houses all over the city, which the *soldati* would sleep upon when not waging war. Contadina, cooking around the clock, found she could not keep up with the hordes of hundreds of hungry bellies and thus hired Sara Leoni away from her midwest kitchens to cater the war. "My boys cannot massacre on empty stomaches," the wise old Contadina opined.

With the war in full blast, Fungi stole out of his cold-water-flat arsenal one night and reported to the Don. "We've wiped out 403; they've gotten 211 of ours," he told his father, who clucked disapprovingly while stuffing Kleenex into his emaciated cheeks.

"All this would be unnecessary if 'The Butcher' were here," Don Provolone said weakly, wondering how his charge was doing in the strange land of the yellow ones.

The village of Phuc Hu a distant and bloody memory, Bonfiglio Bucceroni crawled on his stomach like some deadly viper. Often in the past weeks while so close to the ground he had been bitten by several deadly vipers, all of whom had rolled over and died. After his efficient disposal of Phuc Hu, he had given similar consideration to the towns of Sue Dat, the twin cities of Dis Hue and Dat Hue, Numb Pen, Pinh Pric, Chuc Chan, Ric Shau, and so many others he could not even recall. By now his black suit, yellow tie and grey fedora were caked with mud from the leech-ridden swamps, and his Flagg Brothers square-toed cordovans had become the nesting place for thousands of fire ants. Yet on he juggernauted, leaving twisted metal, bamboo fragments and mounds of gory bones in his wake. Time for lunch, he thought, and took a foot-long hero sandwich from a pail, sat down at the side of Highway 9, absentmindedly kicked a passing water buffalo to death, and bit into his simple repast.

In the sixth month of the Great Peanut Brittle War, New York City looked like a battleground. Unable to avoid the never ending flurries of hot lead and flying grenades coming from speeding cars and empty lofts, even innocent bystanders were listed among the daily fatalities. The *Daily News* reported that only twelve Rockettes had been able to show up at Radio City Music Hall; the rest were unaccounted for. Three Hudson Day Line cruise ships, caught in the withering cross-fire, had gone to the bottom, or as close to the bottom as they could get in a river packed with oil and pollution. A skirmish in the midst of the Macy's Thanksgiving Day parade had sent Allen Ludden and Betty White running for cover to a nearby Horn & Hardart's, where they had barricaded themselves behind a hastily thrownup wall of ham salad sandwiches.

Of course, there were manufacturers who sagely revamped their products to reflect the new gangster motif, turning out His & Hers bulletproof towels and tiny black suits and yellow ties for the newly formed Mobster Little League. Jewish D'Ior, Christian's long-lost half-brother, was featuring in his 39th Street showrooms attractive chain-mail maxiskirts, steel-plated halters, and sequinned Browning Automatic Rifles for the theater crowd who found it necessary to shoot back. One positive thing had emerged from the slaughter. It was once again safe to walk through Central Park; the muggers had long since fled to New Brunswick, New Jersey.

One day the Don, fully recovered—although his face, even with its Kleenex filling, still reflected his ordeal—journeyed in a commandeered Brinks truck, through a route carefully planned to avoid the minefields, to visit his sons. Carmine, not trusted by the others to man a window, was watching "Captain Kangaroo" on TV, still bouncing his Spaulding off the wall. Nicholas seemed to have changed a great deal. The lad still had an oboe pressed to his lips but between bars of "Sacre du Printemps" was firing poisoned darts from the instrument into the street. The Don knew that, indeed, as he had thought before, there was good stuff in the lad.

But from Fungi's room came familiar sounds the Don found unappealing.

He peeked in to find Fungi servicing four society girls a-groaning, three meter maids a-panting, two airline stewardesses a-flying, one Cosmopolitan Magazine editor a-sighing... and his cartridge belt hanging from a clothes tree.

Truly Fungi had gone to the mattresses, but typically he had turned a gang war into a gang bang.

"My son," the irked Don spat. "Momma mia, give your Beautyrest a rest! Your Sealy Pedic has lost its Posture."

A rap on the door caused them all to spin, guns in hand. Nicholas opened it carefully, his oboe at the ready.

"Hi, guys," said a man, doing his best to smile with all these stony faces boring into his. "Remember me?"

"Ah, yes," the Don said. "You are Winston J. Cubberly, the Madison Avenue advertising man, whom we treated a trifle poorly, I fear."

"No hard feelings, guys. We're used to that. Now, here's my latest campaign. We at BBB&R know you guys have gone to the mattresses, but that's old foam-rubber. The up-to-date mobs, when they're involved in all-out war, are going to the waterbeds. Comfortable, healthy, great for leaning a rifle on, and when you put your ear to them you can hear the canals of Venice. A fun product. I've got one outside. Can I show you?"

The Don, finding it hard to say no twice to this little crackerjack of an ad man, agreed to the demonstration. With some effort, Cubberly lugged the already filled waterbed up three flights of stairs and spread it out. This could be quite a coup, he thought; thousands of hoods, each in a $500 deluxe item.

"Well, here goes nothing," Cubberly yelled out cheerily, leaping upon the waterbed, bouncing almost to the ceiling. Carmine shifted his eyes from Mr. Greenjeans who had climbed out of Captain's big pocket and was dancing with a bear. "Oh, you're bouncing higher than my ball. That looks like fun."

As Carmine moved to join the bounding ad man, the Don was impressed. The waterbed seemed attractive, well built, and practical. Lying on it would undoubtedly give his *soldati* more restful sleep, from which he would benefit by getting more gunfire out of them in the morning. Maybe this touch of modernity would improve the Family's efficiency.

A bullet whined through the window from an adjacent building, causing Carmine and the others to duck, but it caught a comer of the waterbed and suddenly Cubberly was sinking. He scrabbled at the sides, screaming for help, and Nicholas started to remove his clothes in preparation for a life-saving dive, but the Don stayed him with a piercing look. "A man who lives by the waterbed, dies by the waterbed." And Cubberly went under for the third time.

By the time-honored laws of the Families, the war was halted for a one-day truce to observe Lepke Buchhalter's Birthday, a custom that proved they were not the mad dogs society thought, but men of true sentiment.

On that afternoon the Don was grateful for the hiatus from holocaust, for his godson, Engelbrute Pumpernickel, was co-hosting the Merv Douglas television talk show from Chicago. "Merv," Engelbrute was saying, "it's so great to be back on top again. The picture has already grossed 40 mil; it got me an Oscar and an offer to do a sequel, 'The Computer That Kicked Back'; I'm having a sordid, satisfying affair with my co-star, Gloria Goody; all the TV nets want me to host a variety show; thanks to Dr. Seymour Feig, the eminent throat specialist who removed twenty polyps, six nodules and two carbuncles from my throat and seventy Gs from my wallet, the old voice is back again, and I owe it all to..." he gazed intently into the camera... "well, he knows who, and for him I'd like to sing this song written specially for me by the Grammy Awardwinning songwriting team of Manny Sheldon and Sheldon Manny."

"Go right ahead, Engelbrute," Merv said. "Sing your heart out."

The Don's old frame shook with pride. "He is paying me respect. A good godson never forgets." Engelbrute leaned against the piano. Two arpeggios were hit... one by the band's pianist, the other, Sammy Arpeggio on 39th Street, by *soldati* breaking the truce.

Engelbrute, who had often emulated the effective theatricality used onstage by the Frank Sinatras, Tony

Bennetts, and Sammy Davises and Bobby Darins, loosened his tie and threw it offcamera. This set off a round of screaming from the delighted females in the audience. A sudden cocky flair came over him and he decided to go those aforementioned worthies one better. He slipped out of his jacket. More caterwauling ensued and he thought, what the hell, why not?, and divested himself of his vest, unbuttoned his shirt, dropped his trousers. The shocked host almost moved to stop him, for now he was kicking off his jockey shorts, but Merv thought better of it. Who was he to stop Engelbrute Pumpernickel once he was on top again? The singer pursed his mouth into an inviting leer and the restored voice melodiously poured out his latest million-seller.

> *Strangers on a flight,*
> *We went to heaven,*
> *Zooming with delight,*
> *On Flight Three-Seven,*
> *Who knew we'd find love,*
> *Six miles up in the air?*
> *Strangers on a flight,*
> *Removing buckles.*
> *While the stewardess,*
> *Served us pig knuckles,*
> *As we munched away,*

(The Don, finding himself suddenly ill, nevertheless held back his rising gorge in reciprocal respect for his godson.)

> *We found that we could care!*
> *Strangers on a flight,*
> *Two greasy people, we were strangers on a flight,*
> *Until that moment when the plane began to drag,*
> *You missed your airsick bag,*
> *Yes, love was just a glance away,*
> *I had to throw my pants away!...*

(At this moment the Don, who had caught up with the lyric, was throwing his own pants away.)

> *And ever since that flight,*
> *We're so excited,*
> *Now when we make love,*
> *We fly—United,*
> *What a lucky night,*
> *For strangers on a flight!*
> *Dee-bee-dee-bee-dee*
> *Your love just gave me dee-bee-deevee-dee...*

"Remind me not to see his movie," the Don told Contadina.

Fungi was treating this cease-fire as a day of peace. His first piece had been racked up at 8:30 A.M., his second at 9, and by noon he had more moving violations than a cab driver going from 43rd Street to Columbus Circle. Nicholas, too, welcomed the respite, spending a quiet few hours polishing his tuba and putting a long-overdue ending to Schubert's Unfinished Symphony.

For Carmine it was just another day of ball bouncing. On the words "we come from Canoga Park and we sell..." he drove his pink Spaulding a mite too hard against one of the flagstones in the garden and it vaulted over the wall into the street.

When he sped outside to retrieve it, a kindly old man was holding the spheroid in his gnarled hand. "This yours?"

"Yes," said Carmine. "I was just on 'and we sell catnip' when I lost it."

"Oh, that's a fun game," the old man chuckled. "I used to to play that when I was a young fellow. Did you ever play stoopball?"

"No," said Carmine.

"You take the ball and go like this." The old man drove the Spaulding off the steps of a nearby house. It flew down the street. "I'm a little rusty, but I'll bet that one was at least a double."

Carmine chugged down the block in pursuit of his ball, the kindly old man amazingly keeping up with him, stride for stride, despite his superannuated appearance. Soon Carmine was banging the ball off stoop after stoop, shouting out joyously, "Double! Triple! Homer! That's five runs for me and four runs for you!"

"Say, you're quite a player, a regular Joe DiMag," the stranger said. By now the two had moved several streets away from the mansion. Suddenly the old man locked his arm around Carmine's neck and flung him into the backseat of an orchid Cadillac that swerved around the comer. "Go, baby, go!" he commanded the black driver.

With the approach of sunset, anxiety suffused the mansion. Carmine had now been gone for four hours with no word. "It is unlike him to stray so far from home," the worried Don said.

"I don't like it." Lazar Pinsky's nimble fingers worked his tabulator. "I don't like it at all. My figures show that Carmine has left the mansion 7,678 times without incident. He is bucking the law of averages."

Nunzio and Renzo were manning the phones, trying to elicit information about the missing second son, but to no avail.

At 6 P.M. Fungi went to the door in response to the chimes, installed by Nicholas, which trilled the opening notes of Mozart's Jupiter Symphony.

"United Parcel," the uniformed man said. "Package for the Provolones. Will you sign for it?"

As in the case of all packages sent to the Don, this one went through his personal magnetometer, then an X-ray machine, was immersed in a tub of water, then opened by Nunzio in a suit of lead shielding. "It's harmless," Nunzio said. "Just a box of Provolone's Peanut Brittle."

The Don took a stiletto from a pocket in his smoking jacket, cut the cord and took off the lid. He smiled; someone had sent him a quantity of his own fast-selling product. Then a strangulated "ar-r-r-gh" rolled out of his throat, his face went white, the veins bulged on his neck. Intertwined with the sticky mixture were many pink shreds, on one of them the word "Spaulding." A chill permeated his body. He knew what it meant. And under the chunk he found a little card containing a mocking message:

My name was Carmine,
And my life was carefree,
But I got careless,
And now I'm candy.

A phone call from his peanut brittle factory foreman a minute later confirmed his deepest fear. "Godfather, two men broke into the plant, held our personnel at bay and threw something large into the vat. Before we could stop the machinery, 2,500 boxes came off the assembly line."

Now the Don was certain. Painfully and yet with the dignity that made him what he was he whispered, "Send those boxes to Babanazzo's Funeral Home. He was a sweet, nutty son in life and true to form he died that way." He hung up the phone and fell heavily into his chair.

In retribution the Don ordered an even more bloody resumption of the Great Peanut Brittle War. Fungi and his buttonmen were more ferocious than ever, launching daring raids against numbers banks, bookie parlors, dope hangouts, which were fairly easy to destroy, because they were all located in City Hall. With Fungi's rising appetite for blood came a parallel desire for sex. In one orgiastic night the awesome *peckeroni* made its engorged way through the Manhattan Bumpers, an all-female roller derby team, whose thick leather padding was no protection against his propulsive thrusts; all the pom-pom girls at Randalls Island; and the entire staff of operators at the phone company's midtown exchange who, after a session with Fungi, found new meaning in the terms *long distance* and *digit dialing.*

One evening the Family sat in the Don's den, fatigued from a spree that had witnessed 716 killings, 568 knifings, and the accidental beating up of the statue of Admiral Farragut in a park on 23rd Street. "Who is not with us is against us," Nunzio had said, crashing his leadpipe against the naval hero's bronze head.

Contadina, her daily quota of 5,000 newly baked bullets cooling on platters, flicked on the RCA Victor Emmanuel color TV, in time for the 7 o'clock news.

"Of course, our big story is the Peanut Brittle War," the newscaster said, "but here's more on that amazing business from Indochina. As we told you three days ago, the fighting between North and South Cheong-Sam has ended, mainly because there are no more people in either North or South Cheong-Sam. But now there's another odd development. There has been no news of any kind from Cambodia, Thailand, Burma or Laos. Why? We don't know and the Administration isn't saying, but something's going on there and the U.N. is holding an emergency session this very minute."

Crashing out of the jungles, "The Butcher," his suit now in shreds, his body racked with a dozen strains of tropical fever, wiped the sweat from his blood-stained face. This assignment was getting boring. He had long ago thrown away the map given to him by the Don (who could read such complicated things? he thought) and was proceeding on his own. A bothersome notion struck him. Was that last batch of faces he had ground into the soil yellow... or brown? Was the epicanthic fold missing from the eyes of his latest butcherees? Had that ungainly homed creature he had eaten been a Thai water buffalo... or a Brahma bull? And why had all those in the last village been wearing Nehru jackets? Possibly because some shrewd Seventh Avenue garment salesman had unloaded this fashion disaster at cutrate prices when it failed in America. No matter. He had his orders and would continue.

Landing a karate blow to the neck of a Bengal tiger which had foolishly leaped into his path, he pushed on, his eyes straining to catch the letters on a roadside sign: Calcutta, 1000 kilometers.

The phone at the Don's side erupted.

"Don Provolone?" The voice was muffled, no doubt by a handkerchief. "We want a peace parley. This war has gone on long enough. We will send a negotiator to set up a meeting with your *calculatori*. Wait for further instructions."

It clicked off.

Lazar Pinsky, after an all-night session across the river in a relatively neutral New Jersey amusement park selected and agreed upon by him and the negotiatori of the rival faction, came into the den at 7 A.M. bouncing up and down uncontrollably, for "we conducted our business on the merry-go-round's horsies."

"Here," he said to the Don, "have a few brass rings. I got hot between midnight and three."

The ever frugal Contadina lifted them and felt their weight. "They will make good ammunition," she said, stuffing them into her bullet-making oven.

"What's the pitch?" Fungi broke in.

"The man, Rossano Mangano, was very shrewd. His Don, whoever he is, was not mentioned by name, but he has been bankrolled in this war by all the other Dons. He wishes to set up a meeting between you and his Don, my Don."

"You mean between your Don and his Don?" The Don said. "Then your Don says let it be Don—uh, done. Aw, the hell with it."

"Where is the meeting?" Nicholas asked.

"It is to be held in a restaurant on 161st Street and Jerome Avenue, called Ruby Begonia's, much favored by the dark ones, who have moved into the area," Pinsky revealed. "But I do not recommend that you attend personally, my Don. It is too dangerous, you are still ailing, and even if you get out alive, your stomach will suffer the everlasting grit fits."

"Anyway, we can't spare you, Poppa," Fungi said adamantly. "If anything happens to you, our Family will disintegrate. No, I'll go, as soon as I've finished fooling around with the convention of the National Librarians League at the Biltmore Hotel."

Contadina seemed pleased. At last her son was no longer attracted to frivolous showgirls and was about to wreak his sexual havoc in literary circles, a definite move up the cultural ladder. Ah, those librarians would soon experience a wild new sensation all over their Dewey Decimal Systems.

"No," the Don shook his leonine head. "You are needed to command our *soldati*."

"But it must be someone with the Provolone name or they will have no respect," Fungi argued.

"I will go."

All eyes wheeled toward Nicholas, for it was he who had spoken. "I will go and avenge my brother's death by killing this dog of a mysterious Don, whoever he is."

"But it will most certainly be a trap," Pinsky said worriedly. "My tabulator shows it by a 600 to 1 ratio. And with all due respect to your courage, you are too young to be involved in such high-level dealings."

"I know it'll be a trap, but I have a plan to even your odds, *calculatori*. Get me a gun and..." he whispered into Pinsky's ear.

At noon on the day of the momentous meeting of Nicholas and the mystery Don, Nunzio, disguised in white coveralls with the lettering "Same Day Restroom Service—You Flush, We Rush," walked into the men's room of Ruby Begonia's carrying a large toolbox and a supply of towels. He closed the door, remained in there for about two minutes, and left.

Ten minutes later a powerfully built black man stepped in, looked around carefully, smiled, reached behind the water tank and found what he was looking for. With one jerk of his hand he ripped off the gun Nunzio had taped to it.

Precisely at 5 Don Provolone's bullet-proofed, reinforced El Dorado stopped at the front of the restaurant and Nicholas, casting about nervous glances, shook hands with Nunzio, who had changed back into his usual afternoon killing suit.

By prearrangement the restaurant was empty. A whiff of hog maws caused Nicholas's fine nostrils to twitch. He seated himself at a rear table and, to while away the minutes, on a napkin scribbled a letter to the *New York Times*, attacking their music critic's review of the previous evening's concert at Carnegie Hall. "I must take issue with your opinion of Maestro Herbert von Carrion's rendition of Schecken's Symphony No. 9 for Piano, Cello and Javelin," he wrote. "I personally found his reading of the largo passage moving and vital, even though it was marred by the javelin that pinned the maestro to the podium. And the al dente..."

The door opened; two black men came in and moved to his table. Coolly they frisked Nicholas, then, satisfied he bore no arms, whistled out the still open door. Nicholas saw coming into view a long, shiny, 1973 Black Panther sedan, with Razor-matic drive, no whitewalls, of course, and a horn that when hit went "honkey, honkey!"

Then a huge black in a white ermine floorlength coat, a yellow felt hat with satiny ribbon, and fingers flashing walnut-sized diamonds towered in the doorway.

"Nicholas Provolone?" the voice rumbled out of the barrel chest.

"I am he," Nicholas said, quivering not a little in the presence of this ebony giant.

"Welcome to my turf, brother. I am Clerow Jackson, the first great black Don, know to my Family as De Godmuthuh."

CHAPTER NINE

"So, you're the mysterious force from uptown who's been muscling in," Nicholas said.

"Right on, Brother Provolone. The day has arrived for total black control of the communities in which we reside. Your Family's day as the leader of the Eastern underworld is over, my friend. First, we will take Harlem, then midtown and downtown, until our stranglehold is complete."

"I gather you are not alone in this projected take-over."

"You gather correctly. The other Dons are more than happy to see me enthroned as long as they get a hefty piece of your father's peanut brittle empire. So you see, I do work well with my white brothers. As a matter of fact, Rocco the Rifle, Tulio the Trigger, Bonnie Parker and the kindly old man who hit your brother were all honkies, which makes me," he grinned, "undeniably an Equal Opportunities Employer."

With a great effort Nicholas managed to keep his face from hardening at the mention of Carmine's murder, for he must appear businesslike in order to maintain this charade. "Shall we get on with our peace parley?"

"Let us eat first," De Godmuthuh spoke. "I must certainly be as hospitable as the great Don Provolone."

He snapped his fingers and Ruby Begonia herself, an alluring sight in her Moms Mabley housedress and Pearlie Mae slippers, appeared with a trayful of the specialties of the house: collard greens, blackeyed peas, ribs, fried chicken and sweet potato pie, all of which De Godmuthuh sprinkled liberally with a hot tobasco sauce that sank with a hiss into the Rosenthal china. Somewhere from the bottom of the plate, the voice of Rosenthal whimpered, "Oy vay, you could die from this stuff!"

They ate, the Don quickly and with gusto, Nicholas very gingerly, for he felt his gold inlays melting and sliding down his throat.

"And now," De Godmuthuh said, giving his stomach a contented pat, "we talk, Nicholas Provolone."

"You must excuse me," Nicholas croaked. "This alien fare has gone through me like Calvin Hill through a hole off left tackle. I must go to the bathroom."

"Oh, is that really necessary?" De Godmuthuh snickered. "Do you really have to go to the john... or are you looking for this?" From his ermine pocket he produced the taped gun, which seemed to set off shock waves in Nicholas. "Let us end this pretense, Nicholas. Your Family really must be desperate to send a boy to do a man's job. Did you think I achieved my dominance by falling for an old hood's trick like a gun stashed behind a water tank? I, too, go to the movies, my friend."

His bodyguards moved in closer, and Nicholas knew that if he did not act quickly, there would be another dead Provolone.

"But I do have to go to the bathroom. Your soul food has hit me like Ex-Lax with a nuclear warhead. Surely, the odds are in your favor. And is it not customary for a condemned man to be granted a final request?"

"I've heard of a cigarette, a blindfold, a hearty meal..."

"Don't mention food," Nicholas winced, grasping his stomach. If there were butterflies in there, they had long since been tobascoed to death.

"But never a final trip to the W.C. I like it," De Godmuthuh laughed. "It has a touch of poetry about it— the elimination before the elimination. You may go."

Nicholas bowed courteously (and carefully) and stepped into the men's room. He flushed the toilet to give himself covering noise, then tapped on the water tank. The lid slowly rose and Tiny Tino, clad in a scaled-down scuba diving suit, lifted his goggles and whispered. "Momma mia, they do some business in this place. For five hours it's been up and down, up and down. Lloyd Bridges never had this kind of action."

Nicholas grinned fiercely. "Good work, Tino." And now his hand held the plastic bag passed to him by his pint-sized ally. He stripped off the covering, took out the small but powerful Japanese .38 automatic, the Sony and Cher, and stuck it into his belt.

He returned to the table. The two bodyguards, hands in their pockets, awaited the signal from their Don that would end Nicholas's life. But before the spidery black hand could be lifted, Nicholas had already completed a lightning draw, sending two bullets crashing into the guards' heads, and the air was filled with fountains of blood. De Godmuthuh threw a hand in front of his face, but Nicholas fired again and again, the impact hurling his adversary to the sauce-stained floor. Nicholas bolted through the entrance and dived into the backseat of an idling car with Nunzio at the wheel. "Get out of here!" And the El Dorado jackrabbitted away.

On the floor of Ruby Begonia's, De Godmuthuh stirred, felt the top of his thick Afro, and grinned despite his pain. The "natural" had saved his life. Because of its thickness all he'd suffered was a minor scalp crease and the loss of a little AfroSheen, but hell, he'd been beaten up worse than that trying to attend an all-white school.

He deftly wrapped his head in a colorful handkerchief and raced into the street, scorning the entreaties of two white slumlords, who seeing his handkerchief head offered him a day's janitorial work at two dollars an hour, plus carfare. In seconds his own Black Panther limousine was at the curbside and he was barking instructions into a car phone. "El Dorado with Tibetan license plates LAMA 718 proceeding north under the Jerome Avenue El. Get it!"

His voice crackled on the intercoms of six orchid-colored Cadillacs strategically located in the area, and their black drivers wheeled toward the El.

Red pinpoints of fire flashed from De Godmuthuh's vehicle, bouncing off the heavy reardeck of the Family's El Dorado. Nicholas brought it to a screaming halt. "Get out, Nunzio, and take a cab. Go report back to the Don."

"But, kid, I can't leave you to face..."

"I said get out." And Nunzio, startled at the true Provolone authority in the boy's manner, complied.

Nicholas doubled back in a bid to get onto the Major Deegan Expressway and the safety of the Mulberry Street mansion, but there at the turnoff was one of the orchid Caddies, a hand reaching from the passenger's side spraying bullets. Luckily, his reinforced windshield took the brunt, leaving great cobwebs of bent-in glass to mar his view. Swerving again under the dappled shadows of the El, Nicholas rammed one of the old green stanchions supporting the structure, his heavy duty steel grill shaking it violently. He crossed over the pavement and crashed through the bleacher entrance to Yankee Stadium and found himself ripping up the sod on the way to home plate.

On the public address system the cultured voice of the Yankee announcer said, "And for hitting your 600th home run, Mighty Moose Monsky, here's a present from the management, your El Dorado Cadillac!"

The cheers rang out from the crowd of 911 people, for even on this most auspicious day the management had been unable to fill the ball park. But Nicholas barreled on, scattering the participants, and an irate Monsky, the lavaliere microphone still at his throat, bellowed, "Stop! Stop! Where the hell are you going with my fuckin' car?"

Aghast, the commissioner of baseball fined Monsky $500 on the spot for subjecting this sensitive Gotham audience to such shocking profanity. Then they all ducked, for Nicholas was making a sharp right, sending players and dignitaries diving into the dugout. As Nicholas made another right, three of the Cadillacs tried to head him off at second base, but the unpracticed trio proved inept at the cutoff play and he raced back to the centerfield entrance. The three cars were not as lucky, all crashing into the right field wall, the impact sending the huge Ballantine three-ring sign tumbling upon them, a ring looped over each battered, smoking vehicle.

Now Nicholas was back in the street heading north, time and again banging the El stanchions while swerving to avoid gunfire. A fourth orchid Cadillac could not match his broken-field driving, blew a tire and flew over the curb into an old film palace, recently converted into an adult theater. When it burst into flame in the center aisle, sixteen men, each carrying a raincoat, dashed for safety.

Splendid, he thought, only two orchid Caddies left! Suddenly he tensed. Toward him was buffeting another car, this one bouncing off vehicles, baby carriages, and storefronts. My God, he thought, it's that cop, Popeye, still after some French connection or other. Just as he avoided the narcotic agent's careening vehicle, he gave a friendly wave. Popeye waved back, plowed through a bus and went about his business.

Then Nicholas tensed again. Toward him bullited yet another car, ramming El pillars, scattering pedestrians and in one instance leaping over a Volkswagen.

That face at the wheel! How uncanny a resemblance to Steve McQueen! Could it be? My God, who would be next? The Keystone Cops? Nicholas shrugged it off and went on his own devastating course.

At Mount Eden Avenue he executed a slick racing change, avoiding a huge truck delivering Wolfschmidt' Vodka, but the trucker was not that lucky. He collided with another truck, this one from a Jersey farm, crammed to the top with baskets of fresh-picked tomatoes. The impact was deafening. Nicholas looked back to see a remarkable sight, the world's longest Bloody Mary stretching from Mount Eden to 170th Street, hundreds of winos dropping to their knees to. sip the unexpected bounty from the flooded gutters.

I'm losing them, he exulted. Then he noticed the sleek Black Panther at 181th Street, blocking his path, and he was gripped by a sickening feeling. De Godmuthuh leaned out of his window, the powerful arm whipped out and hurled his eldridge cleaver, a murderous weapon that flashed in a slanted sun ray and bit into Nicholas's left shoulder. Momma mia, he screamed, in his agony biting through his lower lip. The cleaver had ripped open a six-inch gash.

With his still functioning right arm he lifted the Sony & Cher and fired into the face of the wheelman, thrilling to see it disintegrate into bone and blood. De Godmuthuh screamed in panic; now his Black Panther, a dead man at the wheel, was spinning out of control. It caught the curb, twisted around and rammed into the front of a Daitch-Shopwell supermarket, which had just received a delivery of 500 Georgia watermelons stacked up in a towering pyramid. The front of the limousine hit the base of that pyramid, and suddenly great green balls began cascading upon the roof, one after another. Under the pile he heard the black Don screaming his life away, as the thirty-pound fruits mashed his car into a horrifying flatness. He had one final look at that great face, smothered in a sea of red pulp and black pits. Justice had been done. He who lived by the watermelon had died by it.

As his own blood poured out of his gashed shoulder, Nicholas felt his strength ebbing. No, no, he told himself, you can't pass out now or the last remaining murder teams in the orchid Caddies will make chitterlings out of you. Driving with one hand, he unlocked his ever present violin case with the other, bit off the supple catgut strings, pushed the strands through a loop in the peace medallion around his neck, broke off the crossbar and used it as a needle to stitch his torn skin together.

In his weakened condition, he found holding the wheel extremely difficult. Again he smashed into an El stanchion, then heard a horrible ramble starting at 157th Street, which followed him all the way to its intersection with Fordham Road. Momma mia, he shuddered, the whole damn El is going. He made it into the twilight of Fordham Road just as the structure collapsed with the roar of an earthquake, taking down the whole northbound network with it... Kingsbridge Road, Bedford Park, Mosholu Parkway and the Woodlawn Road station at the end of the line.

When the El went, so did a dozen north- and southbound trains and one of the two remaining orchid Caddies that had not gotten out in time.

All that could be seen in the billowing dust of this Bronx area, which resembled Dresden after the fire-bombing, was a lone billboard proclaiming "New York—Fun City, USA."

Doggedly hanging on, the last of De Godmuthuh's patrol cars battered into Nicholas's rear, driving his car into a ladies' specialty shop near the Grand Concourse, causing a fire and an instant 30 percent markdown on all sportswear. "All sales are final," called out the merchandise-wise manager.

Nicholas spun out of the hosiery department, through the window and back onto Fordham Road, sensing a heaviness in his rear. He had to apply the brake violently several times before the 200-pound woman in the XL-Little Prune Pantyhose was shaken off his bumper... onto her bumper.

His battered El Dorado now running on just two tires, the temperature gauge flashing a dangerous red, he headed over the Bronx-Whitestone bridge, hurling the startled toll collectors a fifty-dollar bill. "Hold up that orchid Caddy behind me for twenty minutes!" The collectors, who would have done a Steve Brody and jumped off the bridge for fifty dollars, winked. "You bet," one of them said.

When the orchid Caddy pulled up to the booth, it met a swarm of picky toll-takers who delayed it for those precious twenty minutes by demanding a show of driver's license, vehicle registration card, by examining the dashboard (citing Article 76-E of the New York State Motor Vehicle Code stating that no orchid Cadillac could cross a municipal bridge with more than twelve butts in its ashtray), and insisting that a wheel be stripped so that the brake lining could be checked.

Bleeding ever more, Nicholas gritted his teeth, felt waves of nausea sweeping over him, but with some strange hidden reserve he sped on. Long Island became a phantasmagoria of weaving parkways, road signs that seemed to sway, increasing his *mal de car*. With a last effort he turned off at Bayshore, and the El Dorado, now riding on redhot rims, just made it to the docks as a boat was pulling away. He leaped from the front seat onto the fluttering white boat and a second later glanced back to see his vehicle burst into a ball of incandescent flame.

All around him were people in casual vacation attire, each one carrying an overnight bag. Nicholas tottered suddenly and fell into the lap of one of them, a willowy blond youth wearing a net tank top over his lithe shoulders.

"Oh, you're hurt," the young man cried.

"Help me... help me," Nicholas moaned.

"Lucky lad," smiled the blond youth. "You've fallen into the right lap. I am Nigel Tremayne, a male nurse."

"Where are we headed?" Nicholas said, his voice growing dim. He fainted before he could hear Tremayne trill, "Why, to Fire Island, of course."

CHAPTER TEN

The *New York Times* carried the following next-day editorial:

THE STREETS: A BATTLEGROUND

Once again Gotham has been ravaged by organized crime. These predators, not content with the daily slaughter of our citizens in the course of what the sensational elements of the media have termed 'The Great Peanut Brittle War,' have now attacked the very physical structure of the city itself. Yesterday's destruction of the Jerome Avenue Elevated, plus the surrounding streets and places of business, amounted to a mugging by a gigantic fist. When, oh when, will these suavely dressed savages cease to use our city as their private battleground?

To which the *New York Daily News* replied in its next-day editorial:

BLESSING IN DISGUISE?
Ho-hum, the bleeding hearts are at it again.

Sure, there'll be a few howls about that socko, exciting, four-star chase that blew down the ancient Jerome Avenue El, but so what if a few hoods want to knock each other off? That's their business as free Americans. By wiping each other out they saved us taxpaying folk a nice piece of change.

And here's the kicker: To raze that entire section of the Bronx would have cost city government upwards of $200,000,000, but these dashing gray-fedoraed Robin Hoods in just 15 minutes made us eligible for Federal funds. Yes, the liberals will call it wanton slaughter, but

redwhite-and-blue Joes like you and me will call
it instant urban renewal.

"It's the other Dons who were behind this Godmuthuh,"
Nunzio reported to his chieftain. "We've got to hit them, all
of them, their leaders, their *soldati*, every last one of them
before they try again some other day."

Renzo looked glum. "Perhaps we ought to make a
deal, oh great Don. We've suffered heavy losses and they
outnumber us maybe 20,000 *soldati* to 1,000."

The Don looked up in surprise. Ah, Renzo was getting
old and frightened. "A deal? After my son's incredible feat
in single-handedly knocking out this upstart mob? No,
Renzo."

"I meant no disrespect, Don Provolone."

The Don let it pass. "Thank heaven, Nicholas is alive.
He called from a secret hiding place, wounded, but still in
good spirits. I have told him to lay low until it is safe for
him to return."

"My God," muttered the CIA director to a shocked meeting
of the National Security Council that night in the White
House. "It's crazy. Now half of India isn't answering. And
we can't put our finger on it. There's been no monsoon, no
Commie attacks, no cholera outbreaks, and yet there isn't
a town responding to our messages. Sir, do you have any
foreknowledge of the situation?"

The President mopped his glistening jowls. "Well, let
me say this about that. I do have some information about
the situation and, uh..."

"Sir," an aide-de-camp rushed up with the red
telephone in his hand. "Priority-Alpha phone call. Code
name: Sausigi."

"Gentlemen, I must ask you all to leave. Kennicott, I'll
take that call. You can go, too."

Alone now, the President listened for a minute and
then replied, 'Tm delighted, Don Pro... um, uh... Provolone.
You have gone beyond the call of duty, done a job that
surpassed my wildest dreams. If we ever have another

all-out conflict, you'll be the first one I'll contact. But one little thing. For Pete's sake, call off your dog. India is still a nominal friend of ours."

He listened further. "Return your favor? You bet! A promise is a promise." Then his jowls dropped. "You want... that? Oh, my Lord!"

But the voice on the other end remained hard and insistent, and the President's shoulders slumped.

"Very well, I'll set it up. And then I'll figure out a way to cover it up. Good-bye, Don." He hung up and switched to the green telephone. "Send in General Rip Kincaide immediately."

With the death of their black front man, the other Dons were forced to come out into the open and dispatch their legions of *soldati* to New York City *en masse*, and the next weeks saw an even fiercer waging of the war. Fungi, now the Number One because of his father's slowdown, sent their diminishing forces into the fray. Between shootouts, he continued his shooting in, nightly steamrolling over all the available female flesh within a thirty-mile radius.

"But you know," he said to Renzo in a moment of rare candor, "I've yet to meet a chick who can take all this *peckeroni's* got to give."

"Perhaps I can find such a girl," Renzo said. "A brave fighting bull like you deserves the best."

"You, an old Medicare reject, can find me a broad?" Fungi laughed, went back to the window of his hideaway and lobbed a Claymore mine into a Good Humor truck.

But three days later, old Renzo, a smile on his leathery face, said, "Kid, I think I hit pay dirt. There's a great chick in town on a cultural exchange tour, Yumekimi Mishigi, the glamorous geisha of the Ginza. My boys tell me she's built to satisfy the Green Bay Packers, with enough left to cater to the Baltimore Colts. She's really got a Super Bowl."

"Maron!" Fungi whistled through the space in his teeth left by pulling out the pins from thousands of grenades. "Where can I get hold of this broad?"

"I've arranged for her to meet you at the St Moritz Brothers Hotel. Here, the key to Room 566. She's heard about you, too. Ah, I'd like to see that... when the *peckeroni di peckeronis* meets the *canyon di canyoneris*."

"If you feel a thrill starting at your toes and ending at the nape of your neck, you'll know the first good thrust will have your name on it," Fungi laughed, embracing his father's trusted old friend.

"He'll be here in fifteen minutes," said Wolfman Jack, MacDonaldi's triggerman, who had shucked off his black suit and yellow tie for the gray-flanneled, crewcut look of a government man.

The ravishing Oriental beauty, splayed out on the king-sized bed, her jet-black hair accentuated by the white satin sheets, gave him a fearful look. "Are you positive this Fungi person is a threat to the Land of the Rising Sun?"

"Baby," Wolfman Jack said, "we CIA guys don't make mistakes. Our dossier says this Provolone has filched the plans for your Toyota automobiles and if not stopped will duplicate them on the American market for $1,000 a unit using cheap Honduran labor. And if he succeeds, you know what that'll do to your economy. Naturally, as a government agency, we can't interfere with the affairs of a private citizen, but if you make this sacrifice you'll be strengthening the ties between your country and mine."

"I can see that it is my clear duty to perform this act. After all, that is the destiny of my family. My uncle, Vice Admiral Hawa Tingzin Groccamora, himself an outstanding kamikaze, gave up his life in World War II by attaching a full load of bombs to the wings of his craft and setting them off. Alas, his mission failed."

"Why?" asked Wolfman Jack, glancing at his watch.

"In the final days of the war we had no aircraft left, so my uncle was forced to use a Link Trainer, which, of course, cannot leave the ground. The net result was the total destruction of the flight school and the Givashita Air Base. The Emperor, of course, sent condolences. Although the act had failed, it was the thought that counted."

"Rest assured your act will be of even greater significance to your people," Jack told her, stroking her long, shapely legs. He hurried out the door, leaving just a crack open. The maiden did the same thing in her own way.

Yumekimi Mishigi ritualistically lit a joss stick and prayed to the swollen-bellied god of the household, Drano, then reclined awaiting her eager lover.

Stark naked, his garb long since thrown off in the elevator, Fungi pole-vaulted into the room on his swollen organ, emitted a heated groan and thrust himself between the yellow thighs. "Momma mia," he panted, going upward, ever upward, for here at last was the *humpo di humpi* he had dreamed about all his life.

Santa Lucchese, was there no bottom to this sweet Pandora's box, and how, he wondered, had it found its way onto a Japanese maiden and what was Pandora doing without it? Stroking like the Harvard crew in its last five meters on the Cambridge River, Fungi at last impacted against the back wall of her sexual being in a collision of unbearable sweetness, and the girl's slanted eyes suddenly pivoted and became perfectly round, for never had anyone been able to penetrate so deeply. And then his Goliath of an organ hit it—the tiny detonator. There was a crash, a ball of flame, and Room 566 was now in Room 666, one floor above. It was all over for the oldest Provolone son. The girl had accomplished her kamikaze treachery—when Fungi came, he went.

"Fungi dead?" Don Provolone's white-maned head fell upon his desk, "Who killed my son?"

The *calculatori* said hesitantly, "I have made inquiries. It was Renzo who sent him on this ill-starred assignation, Renzo, your old compadre."

"I see it all now, Renzo's willingness to make an accommodation with the others. They got to him."

"Shall I order his assassination?" Pinsky asked.

"Not yet. Let us not tip our hand. He will meet his doom when they do. Have you contacted the Dons and arranged the meeting?"

"Yes. They have agreed to come to the rendezvous point. But they will come in full strength with all their enforcers; for you, by calling for a parley, have revealed you are weak and failing, a force no longer to be reckoned with. You will never leave that place alive."

"That is what I want them to think," the Don said, placing another phone call to the top-secret Washington number to finalize the arrangements.

India, Pakistan, and Ceylon pulverized by his murderous onslaught. "The Butcher," his body now sapped by a thousand different strains of tropical bacteria, wandered in a feverish haze, his strength clearly beginning to wane; now it took two and sometimes three blows of his fist to knock down a schoolhouse or a Buddist temple or whatever else was within reach of the arc of his swing.

"Santa Genovese, if I do not press some ice to my brow I shall boil to death in this pestilential place," he growled to himself. Indeed, there was no one else he could have complained to, for the entire subcontinent had been denuded of population by his ceaseless attacks.

There came a day when he at last quit the arid brown plains and, rock by rock, pulled himself with bloody hands over the towering crest that was Mount Everest, kicking over Hillary's summit-topping flag in his animal-like surge to reach the glaciers that would break his raging fever.

Time and time again he bent his head against the piercing wind and the spray of skin-slashing icicles, time and time again he was forced to dig himself out of avalanches that swept down the slopes and buried him in powdered snow, but he charged on, sustaining his body by devouring the sparse vegetation of the area, lichens, moss and several Abominable Snowmen unlucky enough to get in his way. One morning he found himself crossing a perilous rope bridge, which swayed madly with each gust of wind. At every step he expected it to sever and hurl him into the bottomless gorge below. But he hung on, and when he came to the bridge's end, the storm suddenly halted. He could hear the sound of a thousand voices chanting in some strange yet mellifluous tongue. As he moved toward the chorus, he could see a vast valley below of green fields, flowering trees, and white marble edifices gleaming in the sun. Finally, his strength completely gone, "The Butcher" collapsed.

He came to hours later to find himself on the altar of a pagoda, his head resting in the lap of the oldest man he had ever seen. His fever had miraculously disappeared, his many wounds were bound up by cool palm fronds. The scent of jasmine wafted into his nostrils.

"My son," the old puckered face spoke with infinite tenderness. "We have been waiting for you. Our legends told us that some day a tall, mighty man of fair skin would find his way to the Valley of the Blue Loon."

As if to underscore the old man's words, a blue loon flew overhead, chirping its sadly sweet song:

> *Blue loon,*
> *You saw me standing alone,*
> *Without a dream in my heart,*
> *Without a home of my own.*

Bonfiglio picked up a rock and was about to kill the creature on the wing, which would have posed no real problem for it was only 300 feet above him, but the old man held his arm. "Yes, my son, according to the legends, you will lead our people when I die, for the clock of time is ticking away for me. I am the Great High Lama and you will be my successor."

"But, Great Lama," Bonfiglio admitted. "You and your followers are people of peace, while I have consecrated my life to slaughter and violence."

The Great Lama put his paper-thin hand upon Bonfiglio's head, "No one is perfect, my son. You shall learn our ways of peace, share my power with me until I am called away by the All-Seeing Eye, and when you occupy my throne, you shall be given fine robes of saffron, sweet spices and exquisite maidens."

"All these things shall be mine upon your demise?" "The Butcher" asked in amazement.

"All of them. But you need not concern yourself about that now, for although I am presently 180 years old, I am of a long-lived race and should be by your side for another 80 years or so."

"The Butcher" looked at the rock in his hand, thinking to himself, I should put it somewhere, and then, he found the perfect place, the skull of the old Great High Lama. "It is also hard for me to break the habits of a lifetime," he said to the lifeless mass of bloody pulp sagging from the throne, and before it hit the marble floors, "The Butcher" was crying out, "Bring on the broads!" He was never again seen in the Western world.

CHAPTER ELEVEN

"What?" Don Cherri, the Golfing Don, said with ill-concealed annoyance. "Me waste an afternoon with an old 'Mustache Pete' like Provolone when I could be hitting a few down the fareways? Bullshit! Tell you what, Don MacDonaldi, I'll send a few thousand of my buttonmen in case he tries a fast one."

"I intend to go out of respect," said Don MacDonaldi. "Before he went soft, Provolone was the envy of us all. He deserves a hearing, but be assured he will not leave that Godforsaken rendezvous of his alive."

"Dummy, dummy, dummy!" snapped Don Rickeleoni. "I'm to go out to the goddam desert just because Provolone is begging for peace? You know how exciting it is out there—watching a frog give warts to a rock. Nope, count me out, but I'll send a few thousand of my boys, too, just to keep you company."

An hour of haggling ended with the understanding that Dons Rickeleoni and Cherri would not attend the conclave, but that Dons MacDonaldi, Knottso and Comello would, and be empowered to deal with the fading old New York leader any way they saw fit.

The Dons had balked initially at Provolone's suggested site, Tombstone, Nevada, a ghost town so dilapidated that in 1969, after applying for a federal housing loan under Title IV, FHA, the ghosts had relocated in Hollywood and eventually landed jobs as technical advisers on the "Dr. Phibes" movie thrillers. Now there was nothing in Tombstone but the tall, cathedral-like cacti, the tumbling tumbleweeds, and, once a year, Pat Buttram and the Sons of the Pioneers. But in the end, the Dons' curiosity and the fact that they outnumbered Provolone's force by a commanding margin led them to the deserted town.

Radio Station KMPC's traffic helicopter reporter, Skyway Silverman, flying close to the border, informed his listeners of an unusual sight in the desert below, something he first took to be the longest black centipede he had ever seen, until he angled down for a closer peek. "It's a line of black Cadillacs stretching for miles toward Nevada. It's either a classic automobile club heading for a gymkhana or Ralph Nader just gave the Cadillac dealers twenty-four hours to get out of town."

"How is Nicholas?" asked a jittery Renzo at the wheel of Don Provolone's own El Dorado, now just a mile from the parley point.

"I spoke to the lad before we left New York," Don Provolone answered. "He sounded well. Indeed, there was a new gaiety in his voice. This Tremayne fellow has certainly taken extra special care of my son. I understand he is a male nurse, so in reward I will send him enough high-priced accident victims to keep him gainfully occupied for a lifetime."

"Where is Nunzio?" said Renzo, a mite suspicious.

"He is home, watching over the mansion. In a moment so crucial, I would rather have you by my side, old friend." The Don touched Renzo's shoulder. "You, too, should have a reward for your deeds." And so you shall, he thought, exchanging a glance with the *calculatori.*

The Don's car stopped in front of Miss Kitty's, the crumbling old saloon that, years ago, had been the focal point of Tombstone.

In the distance, he could see the great swirls of dust raised by the thousands of enemy Cadillacs. They warily halted several hundred feet down the road and began to empty out their troops. Soon the deserted streets thundered again, but this time not to the sound of spurs and hoofbeats, but to 20,000 pairs of Florsheim wingtips.

Solidly encircled by his enemies, the puffing old Don made his way to a chair in the center of the dusty saloon which sat directly under a skylight, and through the dirty, cracked panes he could see a patch of brilliant blue sky.

"Why is he taking the best chair," Don Comello said angrily, "while we must stand in this stinking saloon?"

"Respect." Don MacDonaldi said. "This is his last hurrah. Let him savor the moment."

A stillness fell over the throng and Don Provolone picked up the public address microphone so that all could hear him.

"My old comrades. We have waged a foolish war. You have lost many good men, I, two irreplaceable sons. And now it is time to stop this senseless killing. If you want a piece of the peanut brittle action, I am more than willing to make an accommodation."

'Too late," MacDonaldi said, not without sadness, for he was of the same generation, and regretted what would follow. "The Provolone day is done. Has your brain gone completely soft? Did you think we would permit you to leave here alive?"

"I had hoped," Don Provolone said, but Don Knottso, showing no respect, cut him off. "There is no hope."

Suddenly Renzo stepped away from his Don and the *calculatori* and permitted the other Dons to embrace him.

"Sorry, oh great Don," Renzo said to his old bedmate. "Fungi was like a son to me, but he was too sex-crazed to lead the Family. And you have grown too old. You did not even have the sense to bring bodyguards. With the blessings of my new friends, I shall be the Don of the East." He let the delicious title roll over his tongue. "Don Renzo Uncola."

"Yes, I can see it was just business," Don Provolone said. He glanced at his battered Swissmake Magnesia watch, with the 17-bowel movement. A hundred shotguns appeared, leveled at the gaunt old face, now even without its Kleenex filling, for in what appeared to be his final bow, the Don had dropped all pretension.

"The time has come," MacDonaldi said.

"Wait," said the *calcultatori*. "May I kiss my Don's ring for the last time?"

"That is respect," Don Comello conceded.

Lazar Pinsky knelt and pressed his thin lips to the Lucky Luciano ring. Then he did an unpredictable thing.

"Santa Colisimo, he has climbed upon the Don's lap!" cried Don Knottso. "That is *truly* respect."

"And so, farewell, my friends," and for the last time they heard the booming tones of Don Guido Provolone, the Godfather.

One hundred fingers moved to squeeze triggers, but then the Don suddenly looped his arms around his *calculatori*, there was a great hissing, smoke belched from the back of his chair, and the shocked Dons and their henchmen boggled to see it rise! Rise like a rocket, which it was, for two Redhook Type-B mini-missiles were powering it up, through the skylight with a crash, and out into the blaze of noon.

The three Dons and their inside men charged into the streets in anger and 20,000 guns of all calibers erupted at the fast-disappearing rocketchair, which was now nothing more than a black dot sending out blindingly white contrails.

"We've been tricked! The old *bastardi* had an ace up his sleeve," fumed Don Comello.

"And a rocket up his ass," Don Knottso said philosophically. "Okay, so he got away. We start the war again and we'll get him. Til see the day yet when his yellow tie is nailed to my rec room wall."

He was not to see that day or any other. From under the desert floor, there came a sharp crack, then a rumble that caused the very mountains themselves to become unmoored, and through jagged rents in the earth came a hideous fireball, some five miles in diameter that turned the clouds into whirlpools of blood. Boiling out of the fireball came a mushroom that in a few seconds, reached 150,000 feet into the Nevada sky, at once pink, red, orange, fuschia and with a dab of chartreuse thrown in. At the base of the mushroom were the atoms of all that was left of three Dons, 20,000 *soldati* and thousands of El Dorados.

The Don had called in his chip from the President and it was a big blue one.

His eyes and those of the *calculatori* shielded from the awesome light by the goggles they had slipped on, the Don looked back at the still climbing mushroom-cloud. "Fungi means mushroom," he said to himself, "and this mushroom is for Fungi... and that pink fireball for Carmine."

Now his rocket-chair, guided by a Signal Corps radio beam, was near touchdown. It landed softly ten miles away, in the heart of the 100-foot marshmallow that a puzzled Army K.P. squad had put together under sealed orders two days before. The Don and his adviser, wiping some sweet white froth and powdered sugar from their black suits, stepped out of the marshmallow.

General Rip Kincaide, the officer in charge of this extraordinary event, greeted them. "Happy landing, gentlemen, with the President's compliments. He and you are even now; it's been a favor for a favor, and he is no longer in your debt. Hence, I am citing you both for leaving the scene of an accident."

Don Provolone took the ticket, handed it to the *calculatori* who stuffed it into an envelope, addressed it to a high-ranking Nevada official, and gave it to the general to mail. They got into a jeep and jauntily drove toward the airport.

CHAPTER TWELVE

With the almost complete reestablishment of the Provolone power in the wake of this daring nuclear gambit, the Don once again found total respect in his world. The Great Peanut Brittle War came to an end; his men took over not only their own territories again, but also those of the atomized MacDonaldi, Comello and Knottso. Only Dons Rickeleoni and Cherri, the last remaining parties to his sons' murders, remained free, both holed up in their fortresses, no doubt awaiting the opportunity to strike again at the Don's life.

But Father Time and Mother Nature, Dame Fortune, and Lady Luck, the even greater Dons who command all men, struck first. One day in his den while granting favors ranging from the repair of a burned-out liquor store to the placing of the next Olympics in Andorra, a crushing sensation hit the old leader's chest and he fell face down on the rug.

Again, the Don was spared immediate death because another conveniently located Wednesday afternoon golf tournament, the Osmond Brothers Classic, at Whipping Wife Country Club in Westchester, furnished enough top-rated medical talent to keep him alive, albeit this time the prognosis was grim.

When the two hiding Dons read of their peer's misfortune, they struck savagely at the Provolone Family, a foundering vessel without its captain. Blood ran again unabated in the streets with each burst of violence, and, by now, New York City's great avenues no longer were designated Fifth, Madison, Lexington, but Type A, Type B, Type O...

When the cardiac monitor suddenly swung into a metallic, but not unpleasing version of "Nearer My God to Thee," the grieving Contadina called for a priest, Father Navarone, one of the big guns in the Archdiocese, and he listened to the Don confess his sins for the better part of three weeks, finally calling in a court stenographer and two scriptwriters from Paramount Pictures, who found enough raw material in the deathbed confession for eighteen screenplays.

Lazar Pinsky sat silently by the Don's bed, his tabulator clicking away, the grim odds ever lengthening against his master's hopes of survival.

"I must see Nicholas before I go," Don Provolone said. "He is our last hope. He will take revenge against Rickeleoni and Cherri and all their forces, for the blood of the Provolones surges in his veins. He will punish them, maim them, slaughter them "

"He is outside waiting to see you, but I have advised him not to come in. The shock would be too great."

"He need not be shocked. He has seen men die. Send him in."

The thought of seeing the long-absent Nicholas again caused a dramatic rally in the old man. His heart, which had faltered almost to a stop, began its rhythmic drive anew, a healthy glow came into his face, and, indeed, he even found the strength to pull himself into a sitting position. "Come, Nicholas, my avenging angel "

Nicholas Provolone swooped in, the effulgent gleam from his patent leather shoes flashing throughout the room, his body sheathed in a skin-tight, rust-colored velveteen suit with a knitted, frilly beige shirt open at the collar to reveal a necklace of Florentine gold. On his head perched a white floppy-brimmed felt hat pulled rakishly over one eye, its band, a brown and white polka dot scarf, hanging casually over his shoulder. On his wrist, which swished madly about in a circle, was an I.D. bracelet: "Nikki and Nigel of Fire Island, the Boys in the Sand."

"Oh, Daddy, must there always be violence?"

"This is the new Don?" his father shrieked in disbelief. "Gottenu," he said in a language alien to his own, and, at that instant, the sight of Nicholas in his flaming plummage did to the Don what all the bullets and the diseased blood vessels could not.

The *calculatori* had been correct. The shock was too great. It killed the Don on the spot. The boss of bosses was dead.

CHAPTER THIRTEEN

With his father laid to rest in a ceremony that had brought out mayors, governors, senators, even a presidential adviser, Nikki Provolone grasped the reins of power in his Jergens Lotion-softened hands. He knew what the next moves must be. Kneeling over his father's grave, he vowed silently: I'll revenge you, Daddy, just as soon as Nigel and I get back from the Provincetown "Basket Days" Festival.

Two months later, Engelbrute Pumpernickel, who had been fulfilling an engagement at the Lancelot Lounge in the Camelot Inn in Las Vegas, strolled through the casino, a lovely brunette charmer in a tight-fitting Rudi Gemreich pants suit on his arm. As was his wont, he was placing a five-thousand-dollar bet here, a ten-thousand-dollar bet there, when he bumped into Don Rickeleoni, flanked by two of his strong-arm boys.

"Hi, Don Rickeleoni. Buy you a drink?"

Rickeleoni looked up warily. Why should this idiot crooner who had in the past been linked in solidarity with the Provolones be manifesting friendliness? Then he realized, why not? With the old Don gone, he, Rickeleoni, was one of the two most powerful Family leaders in the country and Pumpernickel was probably attempting to hitch his wagon to a new star. He relaxed and grinned.

"Sure, I'll have a drink with you, Engelbrute."

"I only seek friendship. Let bygones be bygones," Pumpernickel said with utmost sincerity.

"Prove your friendship by handing over that young lady of yours for the evening," Rickeleoni said.

"She's yours, great Don," Pumpernickel said cavalierly. The girl disengaged from the singer and clutched the beaming Don's muscular bicep. "Oh," she cooed, "you're so big and strong..."

"Let's go up to my suite. We'll work something out, baby; do wild things. I'll be the British in India and you'll be the Khyber Pass and every night my Bengal Lancers will charge right through the pass. It'll be wild, wild!"

They took the express elevator to Rickeleoni's penthouse suite and stepped inside.

On the following morning Don Rickeleoni was found sprawled in his plush bed, scratched to death, great swaths of clawmarks across his entire body, and yet with the ghost of a smile on his face.

On a July afternoon at a Palm Springs country club, Don Cherri had just finished a superb round, when he spotted Engelbrute Pumpernickel at the 19th Hole peeking over the top of a tall Tom Collins.

"Hi, Engelbrute. No hard feelings about the past, eh kid?"

"Not a bit," and Pumpernickel gave Cherri's sinewy arm a friendly jab.

"Glad to hear it. You should have seen me out there today. I had a great 69."

"Don, baby, you don't know what a great 69 is until—" He whispered something into Cherri's ear and the Don's eyes lit up.

"Lead me to her, old *paisan'*."

Pumpernickel pointed a finger at a blonde in a twitchy little plaid golf skirt with an equally twitchy behind. "New stuff, she's sensational."

Arm in arm, as though enmity had never existed between them, the two men walked leisurely over to the girl, eyeing her lithe form as she bent to putt. The trio discoursed for a minute, then Cherri, the girl on his arm, headed for his limousine.

That limousine was found in the bottom of a gully three hours later by a passing Chicano picketing against nonunion lettuce. In it was the body of Don Cherri, his mouth stuffed with Titleist golf balls. Like many a golfer, his long game was admirable, but his putts did him in.

And so, Nikki Provolone, as daring in his way as his late father was in his, became the Don... in his case, the Donna... of the Provolone clan. He was to be feared by all his enemies as the Oddfather, the first in the annals of organized crime.

And the bizarre things he was to do in the role of the Oddfather would shake the very foundations of mob tradition.

But what he did and how he did it is another story, which we do not intend to recount on these pages. You, dear reader, have had enough of our brilliance and, anyway, what the hell do you want for a buck and change?

-Finito-

Glossary of Authentic
Mob Terms

Actori . . . . An individual who has achieved unemployment through theatrical training.

Alta cockerias . . . . Old men.

Assassinatori . . . . Number One on the Hit Parade.

Baleboss foon alle di balebatim
. . . . The boss of bosses.

Bastardi . . . . Where's Poppa?

Buona sera . . . . Sara is bony.

Calculatori . . . . A calculator; a man who keeps the books for the books.

Canyon di canyoneris . . . The Grand Canyon.

Carabinieri . . . . The fuzz.

Cara mia . . . . Back-a to old-a Virginny.

Casa di pussi . . . . A place where they leave it to beaver.

Clapperia . . . . Nothing to applaud.

Compadre . . . . A companion.

Conspiradetta . . . . A conspiracy of vengeance or a vengeful conspiracy.

Corruptos . . . . Elected officials.

Degenerati . . . . A dirty old/young man.

Diarrhia . . . . An establishment that gives you a run for your money.

Doseria . . . . A chip off the old *clapperia.*

Excellento . . . . Right on!

Finito . . . . A little-known brother of Mussolini.

Geritoli . . . . A libation favored by *alta cockerias.*

Goombah . . . . A mob college cheer, as in "Sis goombah!"

Gottenu . . . . My God!

Grazie . . . . Dank-a you.

Hookeria . . . . A social relief station.

Humpo di humpi. . . . . . The straw that broke the camel's back.

Knockerinos . . . . Frontal female appendages fortified by *Siliconis.*

Labonzas . . . . Sicilian war bonds.

Lira . . . . A unit of money usually printed on pasta.

Momma Mia . . . . An exclamation allegedly used by Andre Previn.

Negotiatori . . . . Negotiator.

Numero Uno . . . . Number One.

Paisan' . . . . Son of Tarzan.

Palazzo . . . . Joint.

Peckeroni. . . . . An organ not made by Wurlitzer.

Peckeroni di peckeronis . The organ of organs.

Pipsqueakerini . . . . A pip that needs a lube job.

Racketeer āi racketeeroni
.... The boss of bosses.

Rapatori .... A *degenerati* or *scumatori* who's
                 really in there pitching.

Sausigi .... Kielbasa with class.

Scumatori .... A really dirty old/young man.

Shtarker foon alle di shtarkeronis
  .... The boss of bosses.

Si .... Yes.

Soldati .... Soldiers.

Stupido .... A little-known Marx brother.

Tarantella .... A funky chicken with garlic.

Veedee-eria .... A place to visit after leaving a
                 social relief station.

Dedication (continued from page 4)

WALLY AMOS, BUD MEYER, LARRY MARKS, LORENZO MUSIC, USA MEDFORD, BOB and PAULETTE LEIBOWITZ, CHARLES and JOYCE LEIBER, JIM LOREN, LEE LOEB, LINDA LOURIE, SUE MARTIN, HERB MARGOLIS, JERRI NELSON, LEE and LOIS POLK, JIMMY RETY, JANNETTE KATZ, IDELL RUBIN and LARRY SLOAN.

NORMAN SHAVIN, JACK and SOPHIE ROSENBERG, JACK and FRANCES ROSENBERG, TANIA GROSSINGER, NOEL BLANC, MAX YOUNG, GEORGE COHEN, TED PROBER, TOM DUNPHY, JACK and JOAN CONDON, DAVE and BARBARA TIDUS.

HAROLD ROTH
Of Grosset & Dunlap.

EDWARD D. BROWN
With warmest regards.

HARRY HARRIS, TV expert person, and AL HAAS
Of the Philadelphia *Inquirer*.

FRANK BROOKHOUSER and WAYNE ROBINSON
Of the Philadelphia *Bulletin*.

VIRGINIA GRAHAM, ROSE GRAMALIA, ANITA ALTMAN, ADELE GORDON LEON, CHUCK LICHTER,

ELMER KOGUN, WES GARLAND, MARVIN and CHARLOTTE ZIPORYN, RON PRINCE, JACK EAGLE, LOU WELLS, ROY STUART, SAUL and GRACE BASS, IRV and MALGERT COHEN.

JACKIE KANNON
Of Manhattan's Ratfink Room, America's most dangerous man.

JACK CASSIDY and RONNIE SCHELL
Of "Hellzapoppin'!"

JACK HELSEL, BOB McLEAN and MARCIAROSE
Of KYW-TV, Philadelphia.

GARY OWENS
Of KMPC, Los Angeles. Thanks, Gary, for your many kindnesses, your unflagging good humor, your nonstop mania, and may you be inscribed in the Sacred Book of Foonman for another ten million one-liners. And to your KMPC cohorts: DICK WHITTINGHILL, GEOFF EDWARDS, a walking pep pill; WINK MARTINDALE, of the Sequoia teeth; JOHNNY MAGNUS, the Prince of Darkness, and lovely KATHY GORI, Princess of Shtick.

JERRY BISHOP, a tzudrayteh; LOHMAN and BARKLEY, HILLY ROSE and PAUL

COMPTON Of KFI, Los Angeles.

SWEET DICK WHITTINGTON Of KGIL, Los Angeles, a unique performer, philosopher and phone pervert, the man who tap-danced his way into the files of the FBI, and his KGIL cohorts: CHUCK

SOUTHCOTT, LARRY (MOTHER) VAN NUYS, TOM (THE AFFAIR) BROWN, SCOTT O'NEIL, KEN GRIFFIN. BILL SMITH and DON CLARK.

COUSIN DAVE NEAL GOMBERG Of KYW, Philadelphia, and KEN WEINBERG and LARRY McMULLEN.

KEN MINYARD Of KABC, Los Angeles, an articulate young man, and MR. BLACKWELL, who put us on his list of the world's worst-dressed writers.

MARK RUSSELL The Washington, D.C., Wit, who performs hilariously at the Shoreham Hotel.

PAUL GRAY Premier comedian and a man who said, "Much good conduct is due to poor health."

ROCCO URBISCI Our technical adviser on "The Cddfather."

SAMMY and MITZI SHORE "Brother Sam" and his first convert.

ARMY ARCHERD Of Daily Variety.

HANK GRANT, SUE CAMERON and MARK TAN Of the Hollywood Reporter.

STAN HARRIS, JUD STRUNK, JIMMY BOYD, MILTON DeLUGG, BLACKIE HUNT, MARTY RAGAWAY, ARTIE PHILLIPS, MILT ROSEN, ED WEINBERGER, BONNIE YOUNG, JOEL COHEN, LEAH HAMPTON, BRAD LACHMAN and special thanks to ART STARK.

BILL LINK and DICK LEVINSON Who gave us "Columbo", rumpled trenchcoats and murders and Sherlock Holmes with linguini.

BEVERLEY GITHENS, SAM and PEGGY RUDOFKER, E. WILLIAM MANDEL, JERRY GAGHAN, ARNE SULTAN, IRVING SHURACK, HARVEY KURTZMAN, MEL and FLORENCE CHINSKEY, SAM and JACKIE AROUESTY, LARRY and SYD BERNER, ARNOLD and SALLY BOOKBINDER, GEORGE and ZELLA FITLEBERG, NORMAN and DEBBY FRANK, JOE and RITA FUTTERMAN, BARRY and

HOPE GERTLER, DAVID
and ELAINE GILL, WALT
and JACKIE GOLDBERG,
SID, SALLY and PAUL
HERSHFIELD, LEW and
HERMINE HORWITZ, SAUL
and SANDY JACOBS, DAVID
and JANINE JACOBY, AL and
EUNICE KESSLER, LARRY
and ANN KRUSS, HARVEY
and ANNE LEVINE, KEN and
BEV LEVINE, RICHARD and
MARCIA MEDNICK, RALPH
and RUTH MEHLWORM,
BOBBY and MARILYN
NORMAN, JOE and EILEEN
PERLMUTTER, DR. GERALD
and JOY PICUS, NORM and
MARIAM POSEN, LEN and
FRAN ROSENFIELD, MIKE
and JEAN ROZENBLUM, DR.
KEN and MARTI SCHWARTZ,
GIL and FRANCES SMUGAR,
MICKEY and SHARON
WERSH, JACK and SYLVIA
YURMAN.

RON FRIEDMAN and MICKEY
ROSS

ELIN BELSKY

DICK WEST
Of United Press International, a
fun person.

BOB PEET
Of WTTM, Trenton, N.J.

HOWIE TEDDER and DAVE
BITTAN
Of the Trenton, N.J., *Times*.

EMIL SLABODA and all the
gang at the beloved *Trentonian*,
Trenton, N.J., the world's
greatest newspaper.

SAM RABINOWITZ

JUDGE PHILLIP FORMAN

DR. STANLEY KATZ
Of Philadelphia, podiatrist and
chauffeur.

RABBI WILLIAM
FIERVERKER
Of Congregation Beth El,
Levittown, Pa.

RABBI BENJAMIN SINCOFF

RABBIS HARRIS H.
HIRSCHBERG and STEVEN
JACOBS
Of Temple Judea, Tarzana, Calif.

RABBI MELVIN GOLDSTINE
and CANTOR ROBERT TAFF
Of Temple Aliyah, Woodland
Hills, Calif.

JOHN O. DOWNEY, JACK
CLEMENTS, JOEL A.
SPIVAK, JOHN FACENDA,
ED HARVEY, DOM
QUINN, BERNIE (Matinee
Idol) HERMAN, BILL
CORSAIR, EDIE HUGGINS,
JOHN MARION, AUSTIN
CULMER, KATHY QUAID,
BELLE SCHUMAN, BILL
HART, JACK JONES and the
insuperable AL JULIUS
Of WCAU Radio and TV,
Philadelphia.

ANDY MUSSER JESS CAIN
Of WHDH, Boston, and the
TUB THUMPERS and LENNY
MEYERS

GEORGE SMITH

HERB RAU

HERB KELLY

AUSTIN and IRMA KALISH
DWIGHT HEMION and GARY
SMITH

DANNY SIMON
Our Friars Roasts headwriter,
who taught us the value of
archness, which we promptly
forgot

PAT McCORMACK, ARNIE
KOGEN, STAN DREBIN,
STAN DAVIS, JAY BURTON,
BOB ELLISON, ROBERT
HILLIARD, LEE MILLER,
SEAGRAM SMITH, WENDY
CHARLES.

RICHARD M. DIXON
Our President... and MURRAY
BECKER, Secretary of State.

CRISWELL
Who predicts this will be a
bestseller.

TOTIE FIELDS and her
GEORGES

BILL BIRCHER
Of WTMR, Camden, N.J.

BOBBY DARIN and ANDREA
And the Amusement Company:
FRANK GERTZ, DAVE

GERSHENSON, ART FISHER,
GRAY LOCKWOOD,
JACK HANRAHAN, DON
SHERMAN, ALAN THICKE,
BRYAN JOSEPH, TOM
DAGENAIS, DICKIE LORD,
DICK BAKALYAN, CATHY
CAHILL, EDDEE KARAM,
RENE LAGLER, BILL
HARGATE,

ROLAND DUPREE,
JEANETTE BARNES,
MARILYN SILVERBERG,
SUZIE STANFORD, ??????

RIP TAYLOR
Whose energy could fuel
Rumania for a year.

STEVE LANDESBERG
A brilliant young comic, a warm
human being and "a man who
does strange things with turtles."

LOUISE LASSER
Sex symbol and a woman who
does strange things with NyQuil.

WOODY ALLEN
For all he has done to elevate the
neurotic to a position of clear-cut
impotence.

LARRY GROSSMAN, LYN
SCHIEFELBEIN and SUSAN
FELDMAN
Of CMA

JIM MULLIGAN, BERNIE
BRILLSTEIN, JULIE AMATO,
JOE BIGELOW, JANIE BELL,
DEBBIE MILLER, MR. and
MRS. BILL KEKO, MELODYE

CONDOS, RON CAREY, MEL
CARTER, ZELDA SANDS,
JAIME CAESAR, WOODY
COMBS.

BOBBI RIPLEY
Of The Valley Script House,
Sherman Oaks, Calif.

ALAN KING
A monologist's monologist.

FAY DeWITT, MAURICE
DUKE, JOY HARMON, BILLY
HOLMS, LARRY JONAS,
BARBARA JOYCE, JERRY
LACY, SUSIE McCUSKER,
JOE GUERCIO, MIKE GAM,
NORM GELLER, MICKEY
BRANNON, EDDY MANSON,
STANLEY E. PARRISH, MRS.
WIU LIAM BLACKBURN,
TOM McLAIN, MARY ANN
FREY and LIL BALLONOFF,
IMO MISTRETTA.

LEON BROWN
Of the Philadelphia *Jewish
Exponent*.

BILL LEWIS
Joe E.'s brother.

DR. MICHAEL DEAN
Of San Diego, hypnotist,
semanticist and tension-reliever.

MICHELLE FRANK
With much affection.

BILL GORDON
Of KSDO, San Diego.

HERBERT EDELMAN

HY GARDNER
And fetching MARILYN.

JIM JONES UNION 76
STATION
Woodland Hills, Calif.

ABE'S DELI
Of Corbin Shopping Center,
Tarzana, Calif.

DR. IRVING NEWMARK

KENNY SOLMS and GAIL
PARENT

BRECK WALL
Of "Bottoms Up", Las Vegas.

LARRY ALEXANDER
and MARC RAY, BERNIE
ROTHMAN, HUGH
WEDLOCK, BUDDY
ARNOLD, IRWIN ZUCKER,
DEEDEE WOOD, CAROL
WORTHINGTON, GEORGE
YANOK and MARK
SHEKTER, TRACY MORGAN,
SHARON MILLER, STEVE
MARX, MARK SMITH,
SIDNEY REZNICK, DON and
BEVERLY PALMER.

RICHARD WESS

AL FELDSTEIN and NICK
MEGLIN
Of Mad Magazine

SHELLY WAX, MURRAY
FISHER and CARL IRI
Of Playboy

SAM JACOBS
Of *American-Jewish Life*,
Trenton, N.J.

LARRY DEVINE and BOB
TALBERT
Of the Detroit *Free Press*

CLARENCE PETERSEN and
HARRIET CHOICE
Of the Chicago *Tribune*

FORREST DUKE
Of the Las Vegas *Review-Journal*

JOE DELANEY
Of the Las Vegas *Sun*

LARRY KING

JOHN EASTMAN

ABEL GREEN and NORMA
NANNINI
Of *Variety*

WALLY and AUSTINE
WARREN, MICKEY
DANER, ALAN HARRIS,
ART ABRAMSON, LEN
FEINBERG, ROBERT PINCUS,
GWENDA TALENS, JOE
and CHARLOTTE NASSAU,
MARTY SAVAR, ANDY
FLAGER, BARRY REISMAN,
BOB and JANE AMOROS,
JACKIE HODES, ALLAN and
WALLY PLAPINGER, LENNIE
ROTNOFSKY, DR. SEYMOUR
and RUTHE LEDIS, FRAN
SHANKIN, LEW MARSHALL,
TED and SYBIL COOPER,
WILLIAM H. PETTIT, NORM
WEINSTEIN, FRANK and

SUSIE MARRERO, ARNIE
SOMERS, LEN BOGARDE,
DAVE WISNIA, OLLIE
HARRIS, STAN and JAN
FEINTUCH, LINDA LATZ,
HAL LEFCOURT, LOU and
RUTH DELIN, ALLEN and
RACHEL DELIN, JAMES E.
MAGEE, MILTON and EVE
LEVINE, BOBBY and MONA
COURTNEY, SAUL ROSSIEN,
BILL and LIL HOLSTEIN,
SID and BUNNY SHORE,
MARTY MOSKOWITZ, LOUIS
CRAVITZ, DON SCOTT,
FLORENCE BLOCK WEST,
EARL JOSEPHSON, ARNIE
and CAROL BERNSTEIN,
SAM and CEIL CRAVTTT,
GERRY and SELMA GOULD,
LEN and DEBBIE SHAPIRO,
YOUIE and CHARLOTTE
CAPILUPI.

DR. LEWIS and MARGIE
HIRSH

BOB MARTIN
Of WLW, Cincinnati

PAUL KING
Of WHK, Cleveland

HOWIE LUND and BOB WEST
Of WERE, Cleveland

JUDGE NATHAN J.
KAUFMAN
Of Detroit

RANDY WOOD

SALI HELLER, SID SHLAK,
SAM and BOOTSI COLODNY,

CHARLES TRESKY, CHICK
and GLORIA HALFON,
HARRY BOTOFF, NEIL
LEVENSON, IRWIN and
HERB SPIEGEL, BERNIE
GOLDBERG, JUDGE MARK
LITOWITZ, JULIUS KAPLAN,
ISRAEL (COKE) RUBIN and
ART AZARCHI

HY STEIRMAN
With appreciation.

FRAN WHITEMAN
Of Valley View, Canoga Park,
Calif.

CAROLYN RASKIN and RITA
SCOTT

JOHN RAPPAPORT and GENE
PERRET

CURTIS H. JUDGE
President of Lorillard.

JOHN H. CARTER
Of American Guild of Authors &
Composers.

JERRY GROSS and ALEX
HOLTZ
Of Paperback Library... and
JEAN GARRETT and

ROBERTA GROSSMAN.

KEN GARLAND
Of WIP, Philadelphia.

AL CARMONA AGENCY

JOHN H. KEMPLER
Assistant to New Jersey Gov.
William T. Cahill.

MILLIE MARMUR
Of Simon & Schuster.

BEN STEIN and ED HANLEY

BILL STRETCH and THE
GANG
Of the Camden, N.J., *Courier-
Post.*

LAURA
A magnificent pop singer... and
ROGER YAGER.

JAMES J. SHAPIRO
Of Simplicity Patterns.

JUDY KEITH

YVONNE WILDER
A vilde chcdya.

ROBERT and VICKI LANE

NAT and MONICA
SCHWARTZ

DR. BERNARD and RHODA
AMSTER

WALT and LILLIAN LAMOND

J. WELLINGTON PIDOCK
Of WBCB, Levittown, Pa.

RON POLAO, HORACE
GREELY McNAB,
BOB CRAIG of BOB'S
BOOKSTORES, Levittown,
Pa., SYLVIA BRENNER,
MRS. JERRY L. WAYMAN,
and TATSUJI NAGASHIMA,
another technical adviser for
"The Oddfather."

JAY STEVENS
Of WGBS, Miami.

AL and FRANCES HEYMAN,
BOB and ADELE HOGAN.

RICHARD A. HAYDEN,
assistant vice president;
REBECCA MANLEY, LPN;
NATALINE HEMPHILL, RN;
MARY SULLIVAN, GLPN;
SONJA ROSS, LPN; MARCIE
WILSON, RN; GERTRUDE
KERWIN, RN; PAT LEHMAN,
GLPN; BARBARA E. BROWN,
NA; JOSEPHINE TURPIN,
NA; JOYCE SHOWES, NA;
VIRGINIA McHARGUE, RN;
BONNIE SMITH, and DR.
STARR FORD.
Of Bethesda Hospital,
Cincinnati, a great place to
collapse if collapsing is your
thing.

DIANA FATT
Of KTTV, Los Angeles, and
JACK HANSON

JOEY ADAMS
Of WEVD, N.Y.C.

JOE FRANKLIN and EARL
DOUD
Of WOR, N.Y.C.

FRED GALE
Of WMCA, N.Y.C.

SCOTT MORRISON
Of Mutual Broadcasting System.

SANDY OPPENHEIMER and
MIKE RENSHAW
Of the Bucks County *Courier-Times*, Levittown, Pa.

BEN BOROWSKY
Of the Burlington County
Courier-Times, Willingboro, NJ.

BOBBY GORDON
Of the Friars Club… and JOAN
MAHER AUSTIN MACK

VERA HALDY
Of *Bestsellers*

ALLEN SOMMERS and ABE S.
ROSEN

PHIL ALLEN
Of WKBS-TV, Philadelphia

DR. RALPH COGAN
Dr. Eyes of Woodland Hills

DR. MAXWELL SAUNDERS
Dr. Teeth of Tarzana

DR. DONALD W. LUBER
Dr. Everything of Woodland
Hills

BOB EUBANKS

CATHERINE CAVALLI, MRS.
ALBERT deLIGHTER, HELEN
KAMUF, PEARL FROHLIGER,
SYLVIA HARRELL, IRVING
STEIN, NORM EDELMAN and
SHERRY GROPER.

BILLIE SWINGROVER and
TONI SWIERENGA
Of United Air Lines

WALLY PHILLIPS
Of WGN, Chicago, the man
who swallowed the dictionary
and every morning gives you
a polysyllabic pasting... and
MARILYN MILLER

JACK EIGEN

IRV KUPCINET and PAUL
FRUMKIN
Of Kup's Show, WMAQ-TV,
Chicago

SIG SAKOWICZ
Of WCIU-TV, Chicago

CHUCK COLLINS
Of WSNS-TV, Chicago

RUTA LEE and REGIS
PHILBIN

TED MEYERS and
FERNANDO DEL RTO
Of KHJ-TV, Los Angeles... and
BOB ELLIS, NAT STERN and
PHIL SHANNON

RAY BARNETT
Of KNX, Los Angeles

ROY FOX
Of WLOL, Minneapolis

NICK CLOONEY
Of WCPO-TV, Cincinnati

DON TERRY
Of WUBE, Cincinnati

LOU GORDON and CHUCK
FERRY
Of the Lou Gordon Show,
WKBD-TV, Detroit

ALAN DOUGLAS
Of WKYC, Cleveland

LEWIS K. McMILLAN JR.
Who keeps jazz going

CHARLIE PARKER and
WALTER DIBBLE
Of WDRC, Hartford, Conn.

HOPE CUNNINGHAM,
ROBERT D. CHARNAS and
SHERMAN HARRIS
Of WINF, Manchester, Conn.

JOHN BIRCHARD and GENE
ANTHONY
Of WELI, New Haven, Conn.

GEORGE KENDALL
Of WWJ-TV, Detroit

BILL SMITH
Of WKAT, Miami

JACK WHEELER
Of KDKA, Pittsburgh... The
Manchurian Candidate

TED PAYNE
Of WJAS, Pittsburgh

WARREN PIERCE
Of WCAR, Detroit

J.P. MCCARTHY and HAL
YOUNGBLOOD
Of WJR, Detroit

SALLY JESSY
Of WPLG-TV, Miami

JOHN HUDDY
Of the Miami *Herald*

PAT MURPHY
Of the Coral Gables, Fla., *Times*

JOE HECHT and JOHN
NIZZARI, pianist-genius
Of the Racquet Club, Miami

JERRY WILLIAMS and
LARRY GLICK
Of WBZ, Boston... mouths in
motion

ROGER ALLEN
Of WRKO, Boston

GUS SAUNDERS
Of WCOP, Boston

SCOTT TAYLOR
Of WIFI, Philadelphia

JIM KLASH
Of WDAS, Philadelphia

ELAINE STEIN
Of WCBM, Baltimore

JOE STEIN
Of Baltimore

LONNIE HUDKINS
Of the Baltimore *News-American*

LOU PANOS
Of the *Baltimore Sun*

JOSEPH WEINSTEIN
Of the *Jewish Times*, Baltimore

HERB KENNY
Of the *Boston Globe*... with
thanks.

JOSEPH G. WEISBERG Of the
Jewish Advocate, Boston

PAUL BENZAQUIN
Of WNAC-TV, Boston

DR. STANLEY C. ROSS
Of Van Nuys, California,
"Urology in Rhythm"

TOMMY AMATO
BOBBY ROZARIO

PATRICIA ETTELSON &
ASSOCIATES
Of Chicago

THE NOSH-ERAMA
Of Woodland Hills

DON VAN ATTA, LEE
GOLDSTEIN, BURT RITTER,
SHIRLEY RITTER, REGINA
TELLEZ, JACK FINSTON,
HANK and BARBARA
KATES, GENE and AUDREY
RODGERS, IRV and BEV
PEDOWITZ, ABE and JEAN
FRIEDMAN, LEON, CLAIRE
and KIRK NUROCK, MEL
and MARGE LIFSON, TOM
and BETTY BRENEMAN,
GEORGE and KARIN
BREITWIESER, RICHARD
and MARILYN READ, ALICE
HELGESON, MARV and
NORMA GATES, BOB and
SHIRLEY ROBERTS, BOB
and JOAN STULMAN, SAM
PEARL, JANET PEARL,
LADDIE SCHAEFER, SYL-
VIA WEINSTOCK, LARRY
and BETTY WAGREICH,
JOHNNY COATES SR.
and JR., LINDA GALLO,
JOANNE O'DONNELL,
EDDIE and ALICE GREEN-

BERG, DORA KAPLAN,
ARNIE and SANDRA SIMON,
SOL, HELEN and HANNAH
ROTNOFSKY, ROSE and
ELYSE RUDOW, RICHARD
and RICKI RUDOW, BENNY
and JENNIE LINDENBAUM,
EVA, SID and CHARLOTTE
LINDENBAUM, HESHY
and DORIS HOROWITZ,
CHARLES and BELLA
GREENBERG, CY and CLAIRE
NEIBURG, SID and ESTELLE
LUTZKER, HANNAH GRATZ,
FRANK SADOFSKY, SALT

LEN and NORA FISCHMAN

SANDY BARNETT

PHYLLIS FISCHMAN and
JOSH and JILL

FRED and NETTIE BERK

CLYDE LEIB

RAY HASSON

DON BARNETT, WALT
and MATTI MYERS, ANN
ROSSER, WALT CANTER,
MIKE and MARILYN
ROSENFELD, STEVE
SCHENKEL, MENDY,
WILLIE and DAVE KRAVITZ,
MELVIN L. KARTZMER,
STAN LEDERMAN, BEN
MELZER, MARGE and
MARIO PASCUCCI, MARV
and MARSHA ROSENBERG,
LIPPY and SYLVIA EISNER,
JACK CURTIS of the Latin
Casino, Cherry Hill, N.J.

DAVE HORWTTZ
Of WCAM, Camden, N J.

MARV and PHYLLIS HABAS
With love.

JACK WALSH

ARNOLD BIEGEN, esq.

DR. HERMAN CORN

And WILBUR and the beauteous
NANCY BROWN LEVINE
Of Poughkeepsie, N.Y.

If you enjoyed this book...

...or if you enjoy getting books that you don't enjoy, then look for the full run of Sol Weinstein's Israel Bond Oy-Oy-7 books wherever you got this book. (Unless you found it on a bus or something, because, really, what are the odds of repeating that sort of stroke of amazingly good luck?)

Also available for the Kindle, the Nook, the iPad, and other electronic devices.

Oy-Oy-7.com

www.ingramcontent.com/pod-product-compliance
Lightning Source LLC
Chambersburg PA
CBHW022035170626
46808CB00003B/1205